DOUBLE HOMICIDE
BOSTON

BOOKS BY JONATHAN KELLERMAN

FICTION

Therapy
The Conspiracy Club
A Cold Heart
The Murder Book
Flesh and Blood
Dr. Death
Monster
Billy Straight
Survival of the Fittest
The Clinic
The Web
Self-defense
Bad Love
Devil's Waltz
Private Eyes
Time Bomb
Silent Partner
The Butcher's Theater
Over the Edge
Blood Test
When the Bough Breaks

NONFICTION

Savage Spawn: Reflections on Violent Children
Helping the Fearful Child
Psychological Aspects of Childhood Cancer

FOR CHILDREN, WRITTEN AND ILLUSTRATED

Jonathan Kellerman's ABC of Weird Creatures
Daddy, Daddy, Can You Touch the Sky?

BOOKS BY FAYE KELLERMAN

The Ritual Bath
Sacred and Profane
The Quality of Mercy
Milk and Honey
Day of Atonement
False Prophet
Grievous Sin
Sanctuary
Justice
Prayers for the Dead
Serpent's Tooth
Moon Music
Jupiter's Bones
Stalker
The Forgotten
Stone Kiss
Street Dreams

DOUBLE HOMICIDE

BOSTON

FAYE & JONATHAN KELLERMAN

WARNER BOOKS

NEW YORK   BOSTON

Kel

Copyright © 2004 by Jonathan Kellerman and Faye Kellerman

All rights reserved.

Warner Books

Time Warner Book Group
1271 Avenue of the Americas, New York, NY 10020

Printed in the United States of America

ISBN 0-7394-4758-0

Book design and text composition by L&G McRee

To our parents
Sylvia Kellerman
Anne Marder
David Kellerman—alav hashalom
Oscar Marder—alav hashalom

Special thanks to Jesse Kellerman,
photographer extraordinaire.

In the Land of Giants

1

It wasn't that Dorothy was nosy. She was going through the backpack because it stank. Five days' worth of rotted food leaked from brown lunch bags—a microbe's dream. After carefully extracting the olfactory offense with her fingertips, she saw something at the bottom, partially buried beneath crumpled papers and textbooks. Just the merest wink of metal, but it spoke to her with malevolence.

Her heart slammed against her chest.

Gingerly, she pushed away the junk on top until the object was completely exposed—a Smith & Wesson revolver, an old one. Taking it out of the knapsack, she examined the weapon. Nicked, scarred, rust around the muzzle. Poorly maintained. Six blank chambers, but that was meager comfort.

Her face registered shock, then the rage set in.

"Spencer!" Her normally deep voice had turned shrill. "Spencer, get your sorry ass in here right now!"

Her screaming was futile. Spencer was down the block, shooting b-balls in the Y with the gang: Rashid, Armando, Cory, Juwoine, and Richie. The fifteen-year-old had no idea that his mother was home, let alone that she (a) was in his room, (b) was going through his personal belongings, and (c) had discovered a gun in his book bag. She heard the stairs creak under heavy footsteps. It was her elder son, Marcus. He stood at the doorway to the room like a sentry—hands across his chest, legs spread apart.

"What's going on, Ma?"

Dorothy whirled around and shoved the empty gun in his face. "What do you know about this?"

Marcus grimaced and took a step backward. "What are you *doing*?"

"I found this in your brother's backpack!"

"Why are you going through Spencer's backpack?"

"That is not the point!" Dorothy spit out furiously. "I am his mother and I am your mother and I don't need a reason to go through your backpack or his!"

"Yes, you do," Marcus countered. "Our backpacks are personal. There are privacy issues—"

"Well, right now, I don't give a good goddamn about privacy!" Dorothy screamed. "What do you know about this?"

"Nothing!" Marcus screamed back. "Nothing at all, okay?"

"No, it's not okay! I find a revolver in your brother's backpack and that's *not* okay, okay?"

"Okay."

"Damn right okay." Dorothy's chest was sore and tight, and she gasped for each intake of breath. It was hot and sticky and smelly. The heating in the building was erratic and unreliable, the temperature vacillating between

4

Saharan scorcher and arctic freeze. Unceremoniously, she plunked herself down on Spencer's bed and tried to regain composure. The mattress sagged under her weight. She had a too thick layer of fat, to be sure, but it did cover a body of strong, steely muscle.

The tiny room was closing in on her: twin beds pressed so close together a nightstand couldn't fit between them. The closet was open and overflowing with T-shirts, sweatpants, shorts, socks, shoes, books, CDs, videos, and sports equipment. The blinds hadn't been dusted in a month. The boys had a hamper, but dirty clothing was strewn over what little floor space existed. The area was littered with papers, candy wrappers, empty bags and boxes. Why couldn't the boys keep the place at least minimally clean?

Marcus sat next to her and put his arm around her shoulders. "Are you all right?"

"No, I am not all right!" She knew she was snapping at the wrong person. She was overworked, worn-out, and disillusioned. She dragged her hands over her face. Rubbed her eyes. Forced herself to soften her voice. "You don't know anything about this?"

"No."

"Good Lord," Dorothy said. "What next?"

Marcus looked away. "He's going through a rough period—"

"This is more than a rough period!" She clutched the firearm. "This is illegal and potentially lethal!"

"I know, Ma. It isn't good." The twenty-one-year-old regarded his mother's face. "But if you're going to handle it, you can't be hysterical."

"I'm not hysterical, goddammit. I'm . . . I'm maternal! With maternal concerns!" Again, she snapped, "Where'd he get this?"

"I have no idea."

"I suppose I could run it through the system."

"That's a little extreme, don't you think?"

Dorothy was silent.

"Why don't you talk to him first?" Marcus looked at his mother. "Talk, Ma. Not scream. Talk." A pause. "Or even better, I'll talk—"

"You are not his mother! This is not your job!"

Marcus threw up his hands. "Fine. Have it your way. You always do."

Dorothy bolted up, crossing her arms over her chest. "Just what does that mean?"

"It's self-explanatory." Marcus kicked his backpack over, then brought it up to his arms by hooking a shoe under a strap and flipping it upward. He rummaged through the contents and took out a book. "In case you didn't already know, I've got a game tonight plus two hundred pages left in European History. Not to mention I'm doing the morning shift at the library after five-thirty a.m. practice tomorrow. Do you mind?"

"Don't you *sass* me."

"I'm not sassing anyone, I'm trying to get my work done. Jesus, you're not the only one with obligations." Marcus got to his feet, then plopped down onto his own bed, nearly breaking the sagging springs. "Close the door on the way out."

It was time for Dorothy to reevaluate. She remembered to keep her voice down. "So what do you think I should do? Just let it go? I'm not going to just let it go, Marcus."

He put down his book. "No, I don't think you should let it go. But a little objectivity might help. Pretend he's one of your suspects, Ma. You always brag that you got the soft touch in the department. Use it."

"Marcus, *why* is Spencer carrying a gun?"

He forced himself to look straight at his mother's eyes. Big brown eyes. Big woman; her no-nonsense cropped kinky hair made her face loom larger. Prominent cheekbones. Lips compressed into a pout. She was a half inch shy of six feet, with big heavy bones, yet she had long and graceful fingers. A beautiful woman who'd earned the right to be respected. "I know you're worried, but it's probably no big deal. It's a rough world out there. Maybe it makes him feel secure." He focused in on Dorothy's eyes. "Doesn't it make *you* feel secure?"

"For me, it's standard equipment, Marcus, not boasting rights. And we're not talking about a cigarette or even marijuana. Guns are killing machines. That's what they do. They kill people. A young boy like that has no business carrying a weapon no matter how threatened he feels. If something's wrong, he should talk to me."

She eyed her elder son. "Has he said anything to you?"

"About what?"

"About what's troubling him so bad he feels the need to pack iron."

Marcus bit his lower lip. "Nothing specific. Look, if you want, I'll go by the Y and walk him home. But he's going to be pretty pissed that you went through his things."

"I wouldn't have done it except his book bag was stinking up the place."

"Yeah, the room does smell like a big fart." He laughed and shook his head. "Mama, why don't you go out, catch a quick dinner with Aunt Martha before the game? Or maybe do some Christmas shopping."

"I don't feel like spending money, and I don't feel like hearing about Martha's GERD."

"She's just spouting off 'cause you don't say nothing."

"I talk."

"You grunt."

Which was just what she was about to do. She checked it, forced herself calm. "I'll go get your brother. This is an issue between the two of us, and I have to deal with him. You just concentrate on your studies, okay?"

"Is this going to be loud?"

"It may get . . . emphatic."

Marcus kissed her cheek and got up from the bed. He threw his heavy down jacket over his shoulder and tucked his textbook under his arm. "I think I'd be better off at the library. You comin' tonight?"

"Do I ever miss your games?" She stroked his face. "You need money for dinner?"

"Nah, I still got pocket change from last month's stipend. Wait." He let his jacket fall to the floor and handed his mother his book. "I've got coupons." He sorted through his wallet and took out four slips of paper. Kept one and gave the rest to his mother. "They were giving these out at practice yesterday."

Dorothy looked at the scrips: Each was worth up to five dollars of free food. "Who gave these to you?"

"Local sponsors. They give them away to everyone at the doors. God forbid the NCAA should think we're getting a freebie." He shook his head. "Man, a crummy coupon is the least they could do for exploiting us. Last week's game was a sellout. Because of Julius, of course. He's the star. We're just the sideshow—his own personal valets. Asshole!"

"Don't swear."

"Yeah, yeah."

Dorothy felt a pang of maternal defensiveness. "That boy couldn't do nothing without the rest of you feeding him perfect shots."

"Yeah, you try and tell the hog that b-ball is a team sport. If me or anyone else says anything to Coach, Julius gets mad and next thing I know I'm out on my ass. And there're like three hundred homies waiting in the wings, thinking that Boston Ferris is their ticket to the NBA. Not that it's bad to dream . . ." He sighed. "Shit, I dream."

Tenderness welled inside her breast. Dorothy said, "There are dreams, Marcus, and there are pipe dreams. Like I always tell you, a good sports agent with a Harvard law degree can make lots of money without killing his back and knees and being a washout at thirty."

"Yeah, yeah."

"You're not listening."

"I'm listening, it's just . . ." The young man scratched his head. "I don't know, Ma. I fall for it the same as everyone else. I've got the dream. But I also know reality. I'm trying to live in both worlds, but I just can't keep going at this pace. Something's gonna give."

Dorothy threw her arms around her son. "I know you love the game, Marcus. I love the game, too. And I would never be the one to want to spoil your dream, but I just want what's best for you."

"I know you do, Ma. And I also know the Ivy law schools just love the big black boys with good test scores and the high GPAs. I know I'd be a jerk to blow this kind of opportunity. Still, you think about things." His eyes became distant and unfocused. "It's all right. When the time comes, I'll do the right thing."

Dorothy kissed her son's cheek. "You always do."

"Yes, that's true." He paused. "Good old reliable Marcus."

"Stop that!" Dorothy frowned. "You've been given gifts from the good Lord. Don't be an ingrate."

"Absolutely." Marcus slipped the jacket on and tossed his backpack over his shoulder. "I know where I come from. I know where you came from, Mama. I know how hard you work. I don't take anything for granted."

2

Slumped in the driver's seat of the car, drinking coffee that was too strong and too hot, Michael Anthony McCain squinted through the foggy windshield as his brain took a trip down memory lane, back to the time when he had it all. About ten years ago. When he was in his early thirties, around the time he'd been promoted to detective one. One hundred and seventy pounds of pure muscle on his five-eleven frame, he'd been able to bench-press three on a good day. His hair had been thick, light brown in the winter, dirty blond in the summer. With his sparkling baby blues and his dazzling white smile made possible by thousands of dollars' worth of dental work, he'd been a hell of a pussy magnet. Even Grace had forgiven his occasional indiscretions because he was an incredible specimen of the male species.

Now she had no tolerance at all.

If he was home a minute late, she'd get all snitty on him, giving him the cold shoulder for days even if he didn't do nothing. Which, unfortunately, was all the time, unless he went hunting, which he wasn't inclined to do, being too broke, too busy, and too tired.

Even then, it's not like he went after women. They just came to him.

McCain made a sour face.

It had been a long time since someone—anything— had just come to him.

Fucking-A long time.

He turned on the defogger for the zillionth time, which blasted cold, then hot air, until the interior of the Ford was as hot and humid as a rain forest. As soon as he killed the switch, frigid air seeped through the cracks and crevices, exposing the shoddy fit and finish of the car. He shifted his weight, trying to stretch his legs as best he could, given the cramped conditions. His right toe was numb and so was his butt. Sitting too long.

He was swaddled in layers of clothing that made him too hot in some places and too cold in others. His hands were encased in leather gloves, making it hard to hold the cup, but at least when the coffee sloshed over the rim, he didn't feel the burn against his hands. His nose was cold, but his feet were warm courtesy of a little electric foot heater that plugged into the cigarette lighter of the Escort. He'd be comfortable—relatively comfortable— until the contraption short-circuited.

Given his history with departmental gear, McCain gave it a couple of weeks.

Through the glass, Aberdeen Street was superficially cheerful. The night was still, the air electrified by blinking Christmas lights strung along the rain gutters of shabby frame houses. Snow left over from last week's storm still dusted bushes and trees. Icicles hung like tears from the eaves of the houses that lined the block.

Not many single-family homes left anymore in this part of Somerville; most of the houses were leased out and shared. The neighborhood was no South Boston or Roxbury. Most of the residents were decent types— working-class stiffs, born and bred in and around the city. A fair share of graduate students, too, looking for cheaper housing because rentals in Cambridge were exorbitant. But the district had its share of bad guys.

The yellow house McCain was watching was filled with students, including the bad guy's current squeeze—a pie-eyed sociology major at Tufts. Privileged girl, currently screwing Romeo Fritt, the murderous psychopath. She'd taken her parents' protests as racism. Idiots never learned; normally, that wasn't McCain's problem except that Fritt was wanted for an especially brutal multiple murder in Perciville, Tennessee, and according to an anonymous tip, he was possibly bunking at the pie-eyed girl's apartment—and that *was* his problem.

Underneath his parka, McCain had loosened the top button on his pants, giving him more slop-over room for his gut. Used to be he could eat whatever he wanted and a couple hours in the gym four days a week was enough to keep the almighty spread at bay.

Not no more.

About five, six years ago, he'd started running in the morning—couple of miles, then three, then four. That worked for a while. Now? Fergetit. No matter how much progress he logged up and down Commonwealth, his waist kept growing. Then, irony of ironies, around the same time he started putting on the pounds, his head hair started falling out. *Then,* adding insult to fucking injury, useless hair started growing in his nose and ears.

What the fuck was *that* all about?

He finished the last dregs of his coffee and threw the paper cup onto the backseat. The yellow house had been lifeless for the last hour. He had one more hour to go before his shift was up. Because of the cold, they were working in two-hour segments, bosses figuring it wouldn't look good for the department to be sued for frostbite.

Just one friggin' hour to go, though why he cared was a mystery. Nothing to come home to. Grace had taken Sandy and Micky Junior to her parents' condo in Florida for their two-week holiday break. He was supposed to join them later on in the week, hopefully for Christmas, but if not then, he'd go for New Year's. In any case, no one was home right now. Nothing living in the house except a couple of plants.

Sally had died three months ago, and he was still in mourning for her. The one-hundred-fifty-pound Rottweiler bitch had been his best friend, staying up with him nights when the rest of the family went to bed, stinking up his den with her flatulence. Man, she could fart. Had to put her on Beano it was so bad. Congestive heart failure had finished her. Three weeks of fading away.

He missed her like crazy. Lately, he'd considered getting a new Rottie but finally decided against it. It wouldn't be Sally. Besides, the breed didn't live too long, and he didn't know if he was up to another protracted mourning where his eyes hurt a lot and he couldn't tell anyone how he felt.

Maybe one of those countertop Christmas trees would help—something to cheer up the place—but who had time?

Rubbing his neck, McCain stretched once again, staring across a dark street at the dark house. Nice bones to the place. Ripe for renovation. Somerville had lots of old trees and parks, and on the part that bordered Medford, near Tufts, there were lots of cutesy college cafés. Still, wherever there were college students, bad dogs moved in and did their business.

McCain peered through the binocs. The house remained inert. Fritt's girlfriend lived in the top bedroom, first decent break the police had gotten since the APB came down from Perciville. But not everything pans out.

Fifty minutes to go.

McCain suddenly realized that he was lonely. Picking up the cell, he punched AutoDial 3. She picked up on the second ring.

"Hey," he said into the receiver.

"Hey," Dorothy answered back. "Anything?"

"Nothing."

"No movement at all?"

"As dark as a witch's tit."

A pause over the line. "Exactly how dark is a witch's tit?"

"Very dark," McCain answered.

"You think he skipped?"

"Yeah, it's possible. In which case, I think we should be a little concerned about the girl. True, she's a moron, a dumb college girl swept off her feet by this psycho, but she don't deserve to die because of it."

"How nice of you to acknowledge that. Did she show up for class today?"

"Dunno. I'll check it out and get back to you. I sure hope she didn't go with him."

"Yeah," she said. "That would be bad. How long you got to go?"

"At the moment"—McCain squinted as he checked the dials of his luminescent watch—"forty-five minutes. You're taking over?"

"Feldspar's covering for me."

"What?" McCain snarled. "Why him?"

"'Cause Marcus got a game tonight and Feldspar was next on the catch list, so that's why him!"

"Jesus, Dorothy, I got a headache, a backache, and my friggin' legs are numb. Stop bitchin' at me."

"You're the one who's bitching. I just answered your question."

Silence.

Then McCain said, "Have fun at the game. Talk to you later—"

"Stop that!"

"Stop what?"

"Getting all pissy. It happens every time Grace leaves you alone."

"I can take care of myself, thank you very much."

"Sure you can."

"Bye, Dorothy."

"Why don't you come with me to tonight's game?"

McCain thought a moment. "Fergetit. You'd just bitch the whole time that I was bad company."

"You're always bad company. Come anyway."

"I heard it was sold out."

"I got an 'in.'"

McCain didn't answer.

"C'mon, Micky! They're twelve and one—a shoo-in for the regional NCAA, and with Julius, they're aiming even higher. You should see them when they get it all going. It's like ballet."

"I hate ballet."

"Yeah, that's why I said it's *like* ballet. Stop moping. You'll feel better if you get out of the house."

McCain remained silent.

Dorothy said, "Your loss, Micky."

"What time?"

"Eight."

Again, McCain checked his watch. "That's gonna be real tight for me."

"You're not that far from Boston Ferris. Even though you don't deserve it, I'll leave a ticket for you at the box office."

"What do you mean I don't deserve it?"

"Self-explanatory." Dorothy hung up.

McCain cut his line and threw the cell on the passenger seat. He picked up the binocs again.

Still nothing.

Ah well, maybe Feldspar would be the lucky deuce.

As much as he hated to admit it, he felt better, his spirits lifted ever so slightly.

It was nice to be wanted.

3

Boston Ferris College had been founded fifty years ago, but its campus had stood a century before that. The place was set carefully in New England forest; the Brahmin architect who'd designed it had been mindful of sylvan growth that had taken yet more centuries to root.

The brick Georgian Revival buildings were graced by towering trees and ringed by cobbled walkways. Campus center was a large natural pond, now frosted with ice. Through autumn, there was no prettier place to sit than on a bench under a fanning elm, tossing bread at the ducks. But in winter, especially at night, when the pathways had frozen over, the rolling lawns were blanketed with snow and a sharp wind whipped through the trees and the breezeways.

Tonight the damn place was colder than a meat locker.

By the time McCain arrived, the only parking available was a distance from the stadium, forcing him to play slip-and-slide in the dark, hoping his butt was sufficiently padded to survive one of those sudden falls that hit you like a fist to the face. He slogged forward, feeling clumsy, cursing the cold and his life. And Dorothy for dragging him out here.

Not that she really had. He'd come voluntarily because his home was no great shakes and he was sick to death of lolling around in an overheated bedroom stripped down to his underwear, surfing cable.

The stadium came into view. Decorated with Christmas lights, greeting him like a welcoming beacon. McCain made it inside, got his ticket, went to the concession stand, and bought grub for himself and the others. The scoreboard clock said he'd arrived ten minutes into the first half. The Boston Ferris Pirates were playing Ducaine's Seahawks, and already their lead was in double digits. An electric buzz zipped through the crowd. The air of excitement that came along with a winning team.

As he made his way down the aisle toward courtside, holding a gray paper tray of coffee, soft drinks, and hot dogs, he took back all the curses he'd flung at Dorothy. With his fingers defrosted, he was glad to be here. This was college ball, but tickets for Boston Ferris games were scarce. He needed to get away from his life even for a few hours. McCain was always blue when Grace was gone. Though he hadn't always been the most loyal of husbands, he did value his family. If you didn't give a crap about your family, why bother getting up in the morning?

The Pirates were playing their bench. Giving Julius Van Beest—the team's star six-ten power forward—a chance to rest. The Beast sat calmly, wiping his profusely sweating face with a towel. McCain checked the electronic board as he made his way down the steps. Ten minutes of play and already Van Beest had twelve points and six rebounds. Only one assist, but that was one more than Van Beest usually got per game. It wasn't that the young man was a ball hog . . . Yeah, that's exactly what he was. But who cared? Most of the offense was run through his hands.

Marcus Breton was on the floor, bringing the ball down the court just as McCain made it to his seat—seventh row center. Dorothy barely acknowledged McCain's presence, she was so focused on her son. He handed her a hot dog. She took it, held it, but didn't eat, eyes fixed on the court.

Marcus dribbled in place for a moment, then made his move toward the basket. As he went for the layup, he was challenged and responded by doing a showstopping nincty-degree turn and behind-the-back pass to the center, who dunked it in the hole. The crowd roared, but no one was as loud as Dorothy. She gave her hands a hard clap and only then realized she was holding a hot dog. Her wiener went flying out of the bun, hitting the chair in front of her.

Dorothy burst into laughter. "Did you see that! Did you *see* that?" She thumped McCain on the back hard enough to propel him forward. It was a good thing he had placed the tray of food under his seat. Otherwise, it wouldn't have been a pretty moment.

"Yes, I saw," McCain answered. He looked at the stranger on Dorothy's left. "Where's Spencer?"

Her face lost its joy. "He's home being punished, that's where he is."

That gave McCain pause. Dorothy's younger boy loved b-ball, and he idolized his brother. For Dorothy to lay on something that drastic, it was serious. "What'd he do?"

"Tell you at halftime." She began to chant, "*Dee*fense . . . *dee*fense . . . *dee*fense."

Marcus was now guarding a player who had at least four inches on him. What the boy lacked in height he made up in speed. He was pestering his charge like a gnat, forcing him to pass the ball. The Seahawk center caught it, went in for the layup, and missed but was fouled in the act. He made the first free throw, then the horn blew and double substitutions were made. Marcus went out and the starting guard, a fleet-footed nineteen-year-old named B.G., came back in. But his reentry went unnoticed. As soon as Julius rose from the bench, the noise factor doubled. He swaggered onto the court and took up his position at the side of the key. Van Beest's mere presence rattled the shooter. The opposing center missed the second shot, and Julius came down with the rebound.

A whistle blew. Time out, Pirates.

Dorothy sat back, colliding against the hard stadium seat. "Any movement out there?"

Referring to the stakeout. The question would have been jarring coming from anyone other than Dorothy. The woman was the compartmentalizer queen. She called it *multitasking*, which was the new sleek word of the moment. It left McCain wondering why the young kids today took nouns like *party* and *task* and turned them into verbs.

"Nothing," McCain answered. "Feldspar promised to call if anyone showed up, but in my humble opinion, he split."

"What about the girl?"

"Nothing."

"Check with her parents?"

McCain flicked his wrist, exposing a fifteen-year-old Timex. "As of twenty-six minutes ago, they still hadn't heard from her. What's with Spencer?"

"Didn't I say something about halftime?"

"I thought you could give me a brief synopsis."

"It's complicated, Micky."

McCain arched his eyebrows.

The game resumed.

By halftime, the home team was leading by a cool dozen. As the Pirates walked off the court, Dorothy shouted accolades to Marcus, who gave his mother the courtesy of a wave.

"Why do you do that to him?" McCain handed her a fresh wiener.

"Do what?" Dorothy took a chomp out of her hot dog.

"Scream at him . . . embarrass him."

"It don't embarrass him."

"Yeah, it does."

"No, it don't."

"Yeah, it does."

Dorothy gave him a sour look. "Can I enjoy my hot dog, please?"

"What's with Spencer?"

"Think you can give me a minute of peace before you bombard me with unpleasant business?"

"You're the one who brought up business."

"Nooo. I brought up *business* business. You bring up *unpleasant* business."

"I love you, too, Dorothy."

She patted McCain's knee. "What're you gonna do with that extra hot dog that was obviously meant for Spencer?"

"Want it?"

"How about we split it?"

"You split it," McCain said. "I'm not in the mood to get my hands all filled with mustard and onions."

With keen dexterity, Dorothy split the hot dog, licking mustard and relish off her fingertips. She gave McCain his portion, then bit into her half. "He had a gun, Micky."

McCain stopped midbite. "What are you talking about?"

"Spencer." Another bite. "I found a gun in his backpack."

"Whoa . . . that's not good."

Dorothy's face darkened from mahogany to ebony. "I've never been so mad in my life!"

"You were pretty mad when Gus Connelly bit you on the hand."

"Madder than that."

"How'd you find it?"

"Cleaning out his things." She turned to face him, mustard on the corner of her mouth. "He had a four-day-old lunch in there that stank to holy heaven. I cleaned it out and just saw it." She shook her head. "Micky, I was so mad . . . so *disappointed*!"

"You ask him why he was carrying?"

"Course I asked him!"

"What'd he tell you?"

"The usual crap that they all give. 'It's a bad world out there. A man needs protection.' I just wanted to smack him. After all the talks we've had about guns, all the lectures, all the postmortem pictures! What is *wrong* with that boy?"

"Maybe he felt threatened."

"Then he should come and tell me about it!"

"Maybe a fifteen-year-old six-foot-four boy feels embarrassed about complaining to his mother the cop."

Dorothy turned fierce. "What are you? His friggin' *shrink*?"

McCain shrugged and took another bite of his hot dog. "What'd you do with the gun?"

"I got it at home."

"Gonna run it through NCIC?"

"Probably." She shrugged. "You never know. He won't even tell me where he got it. That's what really pisses me off."

"You want your son to be a fink?"

Again, she glared at him. "Go be useful and get me another coffee."

"Yes, ma'am."

Dorothy watched him go. Fighting off apprehension, she called home. To her immediate relief, Spencer picked up on the second ring. She had grounded him and he had stayed grounded. Good start. "It's me."

No response over the line.

Dorothy said, "Whatcha doing?"

"Watching the game."

"By yourself?"

"Yeah, by myself. You said no friends. What're you doin', Ma? Checking up on me?"

Yes, that was exactly what she was doing. She heard the accusation in his voice: *You don't trust me.* "Well, if one of your buds wants to come over and watch with you, I won't object."

A pause. "What's goin' on, Ma? You feeling guilty or something?"

"I have nothing to feel guilty about, Spencer Martin

25

Breton. I'm just showing some flexibility. Are you complaining about that?"

"No, not at all." A pause. "Thanks, Ma. I know Rashid is at Richie's house watching the game. Can both of them come over? I swear we won't make a mess, and if we do, we'll clean it up."

"Yeah, I suppose—"

"Thanks, Ma. You're the best!"

"There's a bag of pretzels and potato chips in the pantry. Soft drinks, too. No beer, Spencer. I mean it."

"I don't like beer."

How does he know? Dorothy said, "We still have to talk about it, you know."

"I know, I know. Can I call them now before halftime's over?"

"Fine—"

"Bye."

The boy cut the line before Dorothy could respond. McCain sat down and handed her coffee and another hot dog. "Everything okay?"

"Yeah. Why?"

"You have that look on your face—a cross between being pissed off and contrite."

Dorothy rolled her eyes. "You made me feel guilty. I told him he could have a couple of friends over to watch the game." She sipped the hot liquid. "You think I did the right thing?"

"Sure. Not that it matters. You're gonna get blamed no matter what."

"That's true." Dorothy thought a moment. "It really scares me . . . Spencer having a gun. I'm really . . . I'm agitated, Micky."

McCain put down the tray of food and put his arm around his partner. "You'll get through it, honey."

She leaned her head on his shoulder. "There's so much shit out there, Micky. I try to tell myself that what we see isn't everyday life. But with what's going on at the schools, even the private schools, it keeps getting harder and harder."

"Look at what you have, Dorothy," McCain said soothingly. "Look at Marcus! The kid's a shoo-in for law school, probably full scholarship."

"Spencer isn't Marcus. He isn't the student that Marcus is, and being good at basketball isn't enough!"

"It's enough to get him into college."

Dorothy sat up straighter. "If he doesn't apply himself academically, that's worth nothing."

"One thing at a time, baby." The horn blew. Halftime was over. "Can I make a suggestion that we not think about work or kids or marriage and just enjoy ourselves and watch the game?"

"Yeah, that's why sports are so good for people. We can pretend the stakes are high, but really they're meaningless."

"Ain't that the truth," McCain answered.

The opposition brought the ball into play and missed the first shot.

Right away, Julius came down with the rebound and drilled it over to the point guard to take down the court. The Seahawks set up their positions playing the zone rather than a one-on-one. As soon as Julius got the ball, he was double-teamed, so he kicked it out to the perimeter. B.G. tried a long shot and missed, and Julius came down with the offensive rebound.

Julius went up for the shot.

He was promptly smashed in the chest by the opposing center's arm. His body flew backward, and he hit the floor headfirst, a loud thud resonating as his skull made contact with the wood. The crowd emitted a single gasp. Then stunned silence as the coach, trainer, and teammates ran out to the floor and gathered around Van Beest's motionless body. For the next few moments, time lengthened until the clock seemed to stop.

"Jesus, what was that guy thinking?" McCain muttered under his breath. "It ain't a bar fight, you know."

"And they say b-ball isn't a contact sport," Dorothy answered back. "Stupid kids."

"Stupid coaches. I'm sure Ducaine's coach said, 'I don't care what you do, dammit, just take him down.'"

"If he said that, he should be fired," Dorothy shot back. "Arrested."

"Agreed." McCain stared at the floor. "I think he's wiggling his foot. Julius is."

Dorothy craned her neck upward and looked at the giant screen. "Yeah, they're talking to him."

"He conscious, then?"

"Yeah, I believe he conscious. Thank God!"

Two men were bringing out the stretcher, but the Boston Ferris coach shook it off. Slowly, Julius sat up and waved.

The crowd broke into deafening cheers.

Two Pirate trainers helped Julius to his feet. Obviously unsteady, Van Beest looped one arm around one of the trainers and began to walk it off. If Van Beest wasn't able to attempt his free throws, he would be out of commission for the entire game.

After a minute or so, Van Beest managed to walk up to the free-throw line without help. Shaking his head several times, blinking several times, he was off balance and winded.

He missed the first shot but made the second one.

Even in this compromised state, he could sink one, the ball touching nothing but net. Unreal, thought McCain. That kind of talent had to come from God.

Because the foul was ruled as a flagrant, the Pirates retained possession. Immediately, a time-out was called and substitutions were made. Julius got a rousing round of cheers as he was led to the lockers. Marcus came back on the floor.

The Pirate star was out for more than ten minutes of playing time, giving Ducaine an opportunity to come alive, reducing the lead to a single bucket. But then— straight from Hollywood—Julius came jogging up the ramp in his warm-up suit. With exaggerated flair, he unsnapped the suit and, without even so much as a glance at the coach, sat in front of the scorer's table waiting for the horn to announce his presence.

A minute later, he was back on the court, determination and focus etched into his face. He made his first attempt—a nineteen-foot shot from the perimeter— showing everyone that his hands and eyes still worked perfectly in sync. On the opposite end of the court, he grabbed a defensive rebound, took it downcourt himself, and slammed down another basket.

Julius was angry.

Julius was turbocharged.

Julius was unstoppable.

In the end, the Pirates set a team record against Ducaine, winning by twenty-four points.

4

To keep his toes frost-free, McCain bounced on his feet as he waited outside the stadium with Dorothy. She just *had* to say good-bye to her son. The ushers had kicked them out of the building, and now they stood in the blistering chill of night waiting for the team because the coach had apparently come down with a serious case of postgame logorrhea. They stood among an enclave of well-wishers, friends, and relatives, including the middle-aged fanatics who lived vicariously through the team's triumphs.

Guys with no life.

McCain experienced a sharp stab of depression, then shook it off, shielding his face with his gloved hands and letting out a puff of warm breath that drifted over his icy nose. "I don't know how much longer I can stay out here, Dorothy."

"So go home."

"Not until you go home."

She turned to him. "I'm not the one that's freezing."

"He don't even want you around, Dorothy."

She glared at him. "Sez who?"

"Sez me—a male who can remember far back enough to know that kids don't want their moms around."

A back door opened, and the team members began to filter out. The cheering was immediate. Hugs and kisses were passed all around. Marcus came toward his mother, and Dorothy, not one for subtlety, clasped her hands around his neck and hugged him hard enough to crack a few joints. He patronized her with a couple of pats on the back, then broke away.

"Hey, Micky." Marcus was all smiles. "Thanks for coming."

"You had some great moves tonight, Marcus."

"Yeah, it was a good game."

Dorothy said, "How about we celebrate with some cheesecake at Finale's?"

Marcus smiled, but it was muted. "Actually, Ma, the guys and I were gonna go out for a few drinks."

Dorothy's eyes narrowed. "Where?"

"Where?"

"Yes. Where?"

"Ma, I'm twenty-one."

"I know your age. I gave birth to you, remember?"

"We're not having this conversation, Ma—"

"Don't you cut me off."

Marcus remained stoic, but his face was tense. "We're going to hit a couple clubs, that's all." He kissed her cheek. "Go home. Don't wait up for me." Marcus jogged away, meeting up with his teammates, pounding fists and bumping chests with his friends. Julius walked up to him and grabbed his head, plowing his knuckles into Marcus's helmet of kinky curls.

Dorothy smacked her lips and tried to hide disappointment. McCain put his arm around her. "Why don't you and I go to Finale's?"

She didn't answer him.

"Dorothy?"

"Yeah, I'm here. I'm thinking that maybe I am a little tired. And I need to deal with Spencer. I should go home." She turned away. "Thanks anyway."

McCain said, "Don't bite my head off, Dorothy, but I'm thinking that . . . Why don't you let me have the talk with Spencer? Just a suggestion, okay? And think a moment before you refuse."

She gave the idea some consideration. "Okay."

McCain was stunned. "Okay?"

"I'm not in a good state right now, Micky. I'm smart enough to know that."

"All right." McCain took out a piece of nicotine gum and popped it in his mouth. "So I'll meet you at your place."

"Thanks, Mick. You're a good friend."

She leaned over and kissed the top of his head. She was an inch taller than he was and outweighed him by twenty pounds. On a good day, Dorothy could take him down in arm wrestling. She was strong, smart, and fearless, commanding instant authority with everyone from the high-muck-a-mucks to the most hardened of felons. People *listened* to her . . . except, of course, her own kids.

It wasn't that Spencer was surly or disrespectful. He didn't interrupt, nor did he roll his eyes even once—a gesture made famous by Micky Junior. He nodded at the appropriate times, looked sufficiently grave. But it was clear to McCain that the message wasn't getting through.

Spencer packed because he felt in danger, even though statistics were clear that the kid was more likely to shoot himself or an innocent bystander than get popped by a perp jamming a gun in his face.

"You gotta know what you're doing, Spence," McCain said. "Otherwise you freeze, then suddenly the perp's got a weapon to use against you."

A nod.

"You'd never forgive yourself if you killed someone by accident . . . even not by accident. You never get over that—taking someone else's life even if it's justified. You don't want that hanging over your head. So it just ain't worth the risk."

Silence.

They were sitting at the dinette table, the Bretons' Christmas tree a small affair tucked into a corner of a modest living room. It added a bit of sparkle to an otherwise solemn conversation.

Dorothy had put up a fresh pot of decaf when they got home. McCain had just about finished off the pot while the boy continued to nurse his single can of Coke. Dorothy had locked herself in her bedroom but probably sat with an ear to the door.

Finally, the boy spoke in a soft but passionless voice. "You've actually killed people, Micky?"

McCain hesitated, then nodded. "Twice. And the first time didn't make the second time easier."

Spencer nodded. "And it was real hard on you, right?"

"Hard doesn't even describe it. It's anguish."

"But you get up every morning and go to work with a gun in your holster, knowing that it could happen again. Why?"

"Why?" McCain let out a small laugh. "It's part of my

34

job, Spencer. I'm an officer of the commonwealth. I'm required to carry a gun. Matter of fact, I'd be just as happy if I didn't carry a gun. Not for what I do. Now, a uniform officer . . . That's a different story. He's gotta carry a piece."

"Why?"

"'Cause the uniforms are sent into some very dicey situations. Without a piece . . . pshhhh. It could really be bad, and before you talk, I know what you're thinking. I'm not saying that the public schools are picnics, Spence. I understand your position. But you gotta play the odds. And the odds are much worse carrying than not."

"Yeah, you go tell the odds to Frankie Goshad and Derek Trick. Only they won't be hearing you from six feet under."

"Friends of yours?"

"Derek more than Frankie, but that's not the point. They weren't doing nothing, just hanging and minding their own business, and some muhfuh cruises by, talking trash and waving an automatic. Next thing they're both dead. If they woulda had a piece, they might've been able to protect themselves."

"Or maybe not."

"Then they woulda gone down like men instead of being exploded up like they was nothing but bonus points in a video game."

"Or they might have shot up a kid or someone innocent before they got shot up themselves." McCain shifted in the chair. "The thing is, Spence, that no matter how you try to rationalize it, it's illegal. And you not only put yourself at risk, you also put your mom at risk."

The boy's eyes went up to the ceiling. He was saved from having to respond by the ringing of the phone.

Spencer's eyebrows arched, and a puzzled look came over his face. "One of your buds?" McCain asked.

"No, I got my cell." The teen got up slowly and picked up the receiver. "Yeah?" His sleepy eyes suddenly widened. "What's goin' on? You okay, bro?"

McCain could hear sirens over the line, a male voice screaming, *"Go get Mom now!"* He grabbed the phone from Spencer. "Marcus, it's Micky. What's wrong?"

"It's bad, Mick!"

"What happened? Are you okay?"

"Yeah, I'm okay, but it's bad. Someone shot up the place—"

"Oh my God!"

"Everyone's screaming and crying. Blood all over the place. Cops have sealed off the doors."

"Where are you, Marcus?" McCain's heart was doing a steeplechase.

"I'm at a club in downtown Boston."

"Where in downtown Boston?"

"In Lansdowne."

"At the Avalon?"

"No, a new one . . . something Genie . . . Wait a sec . . . Yeah, it's called Pharaoh's Genie. It's a couple blocks past Avalon."

"I'll grab your mother, we'll be right down. You swear you're not hiding anything? You're okay, right?"

"Yeah, I'm whole, Micky. But I'm telling you it's real bad. Julius is dead."

5

Black skies, poor visibility, and icy roads made travel slow and dangerous. The only redeeming factor was almost no traffic this late. McCain drove because he didn't want Dorothy behind the wheel. Even in his sure hands, the car bobbed and slid through truncated streets and makeshift alleys and detours.

Downtown Boston was one big freaking detour, courtesy of the Big Dig, better known as the Big Boondoggle. Decades had passed, tens of millions of overbudget dollars kept being pumped into the project, and rush hour was still a bloody mess. A couple of major arteries had opened, but the planners had failed to take into account that the city and its environs would grow faster than they could handle. Just brilliant. Someone was getting rich off of it. As usual, it wasn't him.

His partner of eight years sat in the passenger seat, her jaw clenched and posture rigid. She was swaddled in coat, gloves, and scarf, her forehead dripping tiny beads of sweat because the heat was blasting full force. McCain thought about making conversation but nixed the idea. What could he say anyway? With nothing to occupy his mind, he began to think about what to expect.

Marcus had been sketchy with the details: a shoot-up following some kind of loud altercation. Something about a girl dancing with the wrong guy, but there was a subtext. Members of Ducaine's basketball team had exchanged nasty words with a couple of the Pirates. Maybe they shot at Julius, or maybe Van Beest had just been caught in the cross fire, this time his size working against him. As far as Marcus knew, Julius was the only fatality, but others had been hurt.

"I wonder who caught it," Dorothy said. The sudden sound of her voice made McCain jump. "Did I startle you? Sorry."

"Nah, I'm just a little spacey. Yeah, I was thinkin' the same thing. Probably Wilde and Gomes."

"Probably."

"They're good."

"Yeah, they're good." She paused a long time. "Not too territorial."

"Don't even think about it, Dorothy. You're too close to the case to grab it."

"It wasn't my kid, Micky. Besides, I have something personal to offer. I know Ellen Van Beest. Not well, but better than they do."

"That can work against you."

She ignored him. "Do you think it was something personal against Julius?"

"Who knows?"

"Just seems odd that he was the only one who was killed."

"Marcus doesn't know all the facts. Could be more people died."

"Lord, I hope not."

McCain took a corner too fast, and the car skidded out on the ice. "Wow. Sorry about that!"

Dorothy turned down the fan on the heater. "I dunno, Michael. I keep waiting for this parenthood thing to get easier. I think I'd rather wait for that Godot fella."

"Who?"

"Never mind."

The car turned silent except for the steady swoosh of hot air coming off the Honda's engine.

Pharaoh's Genie sat on Lansdowne Avenue about a block and a half from the green-painted iron girders of Fenway Park, not far from Gold's Gym. Wide street for Boston, fronted by old brick industrial buildings and warehouses, some of which had been renovated into clubs and bars. McCain couldn't get near the address. The entire block was choked off with cruisers and unmarkeds, ambulances, and lab tech vehicles. Hot white spots overpowered the Christmas lights. Beyond the cordon, civilians milled, rubbing their hands together, stamping their feet. Willing to freeze in order to catch a glimpse of someone else's misery.

McCain parked, and the two of them got out and trudged toward the action. As soon as they got within shouting distance of the scene, a couple of uniformed officers tried to stave them off. The shorter of the duo, a young, redheaded Irishman named Grady, blinked several times, then recognized Dorothy. Even in layers of wool, her physique was hard to miss.

"Sorry, Detective Breton. I didn't realize it was you." He stepped aside to let her pass. "Where's your car?"

Southie accent. It came out "Wheahs yuh caah?" Then the guy noticed McCain, and his eyes got official all over again.

McCain wondered: What do I look like if not a cop? He showed his gold shield. "We had to park it down a ways. When did the call come through?"

"Maybe forty minutes ago." Grady bounced on his feet. "Someone from the fire department should close these places down. Nothing but problems."

"They'd just show up somewhere else." Dorothy pushed ahead. "I'm going to find Marcus."

McCain followed her.

The club had once been a warehouse, its exterior bricks painted matte black. The interior was accessed by a small steel door, making the space a firetrap. As soon as McCain stepped inside, his face was slapped by hot air that stank of fresh blood and gunpowder. It was chaos, police personnel desperately trying to calm down horrified witnesses while EMTs tended to the wounded. A young black man was lying on the floor facedown, hands cuffed behind his back, guarded by four uniformed officers because the kid was a very big boy.

Dorothy quickly scanned the room, trying to spot Marcus, but the crowd was thick and the lighting was poor. The walls had also been painted black, with purple Day-Glo up lighting that provided spooky, fun-house illumination. There was some reflection from the long, mirror-backed bar that ran along the eastern wall, but it was more for atmosphere than clarity. The room was crammed with people, upturned tables, and lots of chairs. Two fifteen-foot-high aluminum Christmas trees framed the bandstand, twinkling Tivoli lights adding to the sense of the surreal. Some of the trees' elaborate ornaments had fallen and shattered on the dance floor. Paramedics had cleared open areas and were tending to the wounded and the shocked.

A VIP mezzanine ringed its way above the lower level. The elevated story had its own bars and its own waitresses. Instead of backless stools or wooden director's chairs, it had plush velvet couches and love seats. The tier was the site of intense tech activity. Even at this distance, McCain could spot a dangling arm.

He exchanged looks with his partner. Dorothy's eyes welled up with tears. "I dunno if I'm ready for it. You go up there. Let me find Marcus first."

"Good idea." McCain gave her shoulder a firm squeeze, then headed for the stairwell. The elevator had been roped off with yellow crime scene tape. As he approached the hub, his stomach started churning. The hot dog he'd eaten at the game laser-sliced through his gut. What was *that* all about? He pushed through the crowd until he was afforded a clear view. Swallowing to keep from retching.

Three hours ago, this boy had played the game of his life. Now the handsome face of Julius Van Beest was waxen and soulless.

Eyes without light, mouth open, rivulets of blood dripping down the left temple. The kid had taken hits to his head, right arm, right shoulder.

McCain felt someone touch his back, and he jumped, pivoting. Cory Wilde was holding an evidence bag, looking guarded.

Wilde was in his mid-thirties, a balding man with a bland face except for having one green eye and one brown eye. As a result, he seemed asymmetrical.

"What are you doin' here, Micky?"

"Keeping my partner company. Her kid's here. He called her up."

"No shit! Who is he?"

"Marcus Breton, BF guard."

A shake of the head. "I've been busy up here."

"What happened?" McCain asked.

Wilde glanced at the body. "We got a shooter cuffed downstairs."

"I saw. What was the flash point?"

"Some argument about the game." Wilde rubbed his nose against his shoulder because his hands were latex-gloved. "You were at the game?"

"Me and Dorothy both."

"Somebody clobbered Julius on court?"

"Someone fouled him hard. He the shooter?"

"I dunno if it was him personally, 'cause I wasn't at the game. But it looks like the teams took it off the court. Lot of name-calling. Then when Julius made a move on a girl, there was a scuffle. The bouncers broke it up. The offending party left and everything was fine and peaceful, la-di-da. Then the OP comes back with a couple of buddies and, *bam,* bullets start flying."

"He came back looking for Julius?"

"Looks that way. If you see the way he fell down . . . C'mere." Wilde took McCain over to the body. He took his gloved hand and stuck his pinkie into an elongated bullet hole on Julius's shoulder. "You can feel the upward path of the trajectory. Now, anyone shooting towards the big guy's head would have to shoot upward. But this angle's pretty damn steep." He took his finger out. "Wanna see for yourself?"

"I'll take your word for it."

"Has to be that the bullets came from below and were fired upward. And that isn't the picture we're getting from the witnesses."

McCain bent down and sniffed the wound. No strong odor of gunpowder leaked from the man's clothing—consistent with a long-range shot. "Julius the only fatality?"

"So far, yes. Paramedics have taken a couple of people who look to be in fairly serious condition, but they was talkin' on the gurneys—a good sign."

McCain nodded. "What's the name of the sweetheart who shot Julius?"

"B-baller named Delveccio. Guy's got a very hard attitude, and he's not saying anything except for you know what."

"'I didn't do *nothin'.*'"

"What else?" said Wilde. "When the bullets started, there was mass panic. Asshole claims he was just there, someone else did the shootings, the only reason he was singled out was because he was from Ducaine." Wilde frowned. "When we searched him, we didn't find a weapon."

"Find it anywhere else?"

"Hey," said Wilde. "You must be a detective. Yeah, that's the problem. We found weapons. As in plural. Lots of weapons." He shook his head. "It's like every idiot in the place was packing. Man, this one's gonna take up lots of time. It would sure make it easier if someone confessed."

McCain nodded. He knew the drill. Detectives would go through the confiscated firearms and try to pair each weapon to its owner using gun ID numbers—if they hadn't been filed or acid-burned off—state reg numbers, latent prints. But prints were often hard to pull from a fired weapon, because when a gun was discharged, hands jerked and slid and stuff got smudged. Even so, Ballistics would be required to discharge each recovered firearm into gelatin blocks to get the tool markings. Hopefully, one set of markings would line up with the fatal bullet. It was tedious, tedious business.

"I'll help if you want."

"That'd be a good thing." Wilde held up the paper evidence bag. "I'm gonna take these bullets over to the lab as soon as the ME's done. Gomes found some casings downstairs where we think the perp fired off his rounds. The angle looks good, but the shooting team will let us know for sure. Where's Dorothy's kid?"

"With the other witnesses."

"I'll go talk to him."

"Why don't you let me do it, Cory?"

Wilde looked at him. "You're a little close to this, Micky."

"I can get more out of him than you can."

Wilde snorted. Gave it some thought. "Not with Dorothy around."

He was right, but it was going to be a trick to separate Mama Lion from her cub.

"I got an idea, Wilde. Why don't you take the bullets over to Ballistics and get some shut-eye and Dorothy will wait for the ME. She'll bring you up to speed in the morning."

"That ain't protocol, Micky. What's she looking to get out of this?"

"She knows the mother—Ellen Van Beest."

Wilde considered that. "You're saying she definitely wants in?"

"I'm just making an educated guess about my partner."

"And you?"

"We're partners. Here's the deal: I'll help you mix and match weapons. And the sooner you get the rounds over to Ballistics, the sooner we'll have information on the type of weapon fired. It'll narrow down the search. Meanwhile, you can catch some shut-eye. You look like shit."

Wilde glared. "Sure. Send her up here."

"You could do worse," said McCain. "Dorothy has a nose for reconstructing crime scenes."

"Well, we need something. Man, it's nothing but confusion." Wilde shook his head. "So either you or her will let me know what the ME says?"

"You bet."

McCain stared down at Julius Van Beest's lifeless body.

Like he needed a doc to tell him that the poor bastard had been shot to death.

6

Dorothy Breton was a big woman, but it took McCain over ten minutes to find her. Interspersed in the throng were much bigger people: the giants of college basketball. They loomed over Dorothy, making her appear average height. Still, she was a presence, and it was her voice that McCain homed in on.

She was sitting at the bar, a hand on Marcus's arm. A gesture of comfort, but it did little to calm the boy. His face was raw pain. He was shouting at her.

"I keep telling you I don't remember, Mama! Why do you keep going over it again and again?"

"Because every time we talk, you remember more than you think."

McCain elbowed his way through the crowd and took the seat next to his partner. "You're wanted upstairs," he told Dorothy. She threw him a puzzled look. "I told Wilde you'd be there when the ME came. No one's bagged the hands yet."

"You notice any powder residue?"

"Couldn't see a damn thing in this lighting, but I didn't smell it. Still, we need to assume and make sure. If the shysters go for the self-defense angle, and no one checked his hands for powder, we're gonna look like asses."

"Did you find a discharged weapon near him?"

"No, but there was a couple of shells in the area. Could be old ones, but we gotta check it all out."

"So there is a possibility that Van Beest shot back . . . or shot first."

"It's possible." McCain shrugged. "Anyway, Wilde just left to take the ammo down to Ballistics. The bad boys look like .32 caliber."

"How many?"

"Four, I think."

"Any other victims in that area other than Julius?"

"Not that I could tell," McCain said.

"So someone unloaded on him."

"We were told that there was conflict between Julius and one of the Ducaine players. The offending person left and returned later, spoiling for a battle. We don't know who shot first or if Julius shot at all. That's why we gotta go up there and bag the hands before the ME comes."

"Why didn't you do it?" Dorothy asked. "I'm busy."

"I'll take over what you're doing."

Dorothy glared. McCain shrugged her off. "I told Wilde that you got a nose for crime scenes. He said to send you upstairs and look around."

"I got a nose for bullshit. Someone's trying to get rid of me."

McCain didn't answer. Dorothy frowned and got up from her seat. As she walked away, she looked over her shoulder at her son. "I'll deal with you later."

"Goddamn!" Marcus swore out loud after his mother was gone. "What does she want from me? I didn't see anything!"

McCain put his hand on the young boy's shoulder. "Maternal concern."

"Fuck, I'm concerned, too." The kid was yelling. "I'd help if I could, but I hit the ground just like everyone else after the shooting started." Marcus's eyes narrowed in defiance. "Can I go now?"

"Give me a few minutes."

The boy's eyes rolled to the back of his head.

"C'mon, indulge me, Marcus." McCain stood up. "Let's take a walk. Looks like you could use some air."

Marcus didn't respond. Then, abruptly, he shot to his feet and grabbed his overcoat. "Anything to get the hell out of here."

The deputy medical examiner was a child, although in Dorothy's perception everyone under fifty was a child. But this one really was a baby with her fresh white face and her big, round "omigosh" blue eyes and her skinny body and little skinny wrists that were covered by latex gloves. Expensive coat, looked like cashmere or at least a blend.

Obviously a virgin, 'cause after you messed up a nice piece of threads on human body fluids, you learned.

Dorothy walked up and introduced herself as Detective Breton from Boston Homicide, and the little girl said she was Tiffany Artles. "MD" on her name tag, but she was not using the title. Like she was embarrassed. Or patronizing.

All that did was further piss Dorothy off. If you're a goddamn doctor with a goddamn degree, use your goddamn title. She wasn't goddamn threatened.

Stupid people. Though for all she knew, Tiffany Artles's MD was from Hah-vuhd.

It just showed how the city, as liberal as it was, really didn't give a rat's ass about the death of a black boy. If it did, no green-around-the-ears cashmere coat would've been sent.

Look at her, actually shaking as she opened her doctor's bag. Of course, it didn't help that Dorothy was glaring at her. She knew she wasn't being fair, but she didn't give a damn about that, either.

"Has the shooting team been down here yet?" Artles asked.

Little, tinkling voice. Smooth, shiny chestnut hair. It took all of Dorothy's will not to mimic her.

"No, I don't think so. Not that anyone would tell me anything."

"Okay." Artles's voice rose even higher. "I just wanted to know if I should move the body or—"

"The paramedics did CPR," Dorothy snapped. "His shirt is open, and those are bruise marks on the chest. They obviously tried to revive him. They must have moved him at that time, because the splatter patterns are not consistent with the position of the body. See here . . . all the blood on the tabletop. Looks to me like he fell forward, and then the EMTs turned him over. I know the photographer has come and gone. So just do what you need to do."

Dr. Tiffany regarded Julius's inert body. Her lip curled. "I'm sorry. I must look like a doofus. I just didn't expect to recognize the victim."

"They didn't tell you who it was?"

"No. Just that there was a shooting in Pharaoh's Genie and there was a fatality." She looked at Dorothy. "I saw him play a week ago. I took my younger sister to the game. What a waste!"

She bent down. "Okay." Talking to herself. "Let's see what we've got."

Dorothy kneeled next to the young woman, who cradled Julius's head, then moved it to the side to scrutinize the gunshots at the temple. "Two graze wounds. They run into one another, but you can see two distinct ellipses. The right one's a bit deeper than the left, but to my eye, it doesn't look like either is the cause of death. There is bleeding, but it's not excessive, not like you'd see in arterial bleeding."

She lifted Julius's limp arm.

"No rigor, obviously. No way there'd be, this soon . . . When did the call come in, Detective?"

"About an hour ago. Maybe a little longer."

"So time of death isn't in question." Artles examined the arm. "There are two bullet wounds in the arm. In and out and not at close range. I'd say judging by the entrance wound, the distance was in the fifty-to-seventy-feet range. To hit him in the head, the shooter must have been good or lucky or both and have had a clear field. No one else was killed, right?"

"No."

"The size of the holes . . . I'd say a thirty-two, something like that." She focused her blue eyes.

"You'd be right. Detective Wilde is taking the ammo down to Ballistics as we speak. We found some shells down below." Dorothy stood up and pointed. "Right there, at the left-hand corner of the dance floor. So we're talking maybe a forty-five-degree trajectory."

"I'll measure the angle of the pathway between entrance and exit wound, see if you're on target. This shot"—she showed the wound to Dorothy—"this one tore through the muscle, so I don't really have a clean tunnel to work with. But the bottom one was in and out." She lowered his arm. "As far as his shoulder wound, the bullet appears to have entered right under his armpit, went behind the scapula, and . . ." With effort, she lifted up Van Beest's body just enough to peek under him. "Oh . . . it came out here, through the back of the neck. It probably blasted through the carotid. Although there's not a lot of lividity, pooling of the blood due to gravity—"

Tiffany Artles stopped herself. "You know what lividity is."

Finally, Dorothy graced her with a smile. "Go on, honey, you're doing fine."

Tiffany smiled full force. "This is my second day on the job, Detective Breton. I guarantee you that if the powers-that-be had known it was someone semifamous, they would have called a senior ME."

"But who cares if it's just another black boy being shot up?"

"It's not that, Detective. White or black, this was called in as a case where the cause of death was easily determined. There was no need to wake up the boss. Except when it comes to someone famous . . . someone who might make the papers."

She stood up and snapped off her gloves. "I can't say for sure which shot was the fatal one until he's opened up."

"When do you think that'll be?"

"Probably soon because of who he is . . . was. I'd say maybe two to three hours. They'll want to dispose of the autopsy quickly because the papers will want answers." She gave Dorothy her card. "I don't know if I'll be doing the cutting. I suspect not. But you can call me anyway."

"Thank you, Doctor."

Tiffany smiled weakly. "So I'll tell the guys in the wagon to take him to the morgue—unless you need to examine him for forensics."

"Techs and I checked out what we needed. Photographer has the postmortem shots." As Dorothy got to her feet, her kneecaps cracked. "How about we let the poor boy rest in private?"

7

McCain walked Marcus through the club and out. The air was bitter, burning McCain's throat and lungs with each inhalation. Flashes of light danced through the inky sky, from the blinking strobe bars atop emergency vehicles, the hazy streetlamps, cops' flashlights, the intrusive winks of cameras. McCain hadn't walked more than a few steps before a microphone was shoved in his face.

That Hudson guy—night-shift drone on one of the local stations.

"Derek Hudson, Detective. Can you tell us what's going on inside?"

McCain regretted keeping his shield pinned to his coat. "Not really." He pulled the brim of his cap over his ears and kept a firm hand on Marcus's arm while scanning the area for an empty cruiser.

Just as McCain got past Hudson, a young woman pushed her way to the front, a face McCain didn't recognize. She was covered head to toe in outerwear and had to lower the scarf around her mouth to talk. "Liz Mantell from CNN. We've seen lots of gunshot victims being taken away on stretchers. What led up to the shootings, Detective?"

Her teeth were chattering as she spoke. A minute of exposure and already the bottoms of McCain's feet felt like ice. And this without winds coming off the Back Bay. Even in the dim light, the reporter's nose was bright red. McCain felt sorry for her, shivering in single-digit temperatures. But not that sorry.

"No comment."

She tagged along. "So there definitely was a multiple shooting?"

"Nothing has been confirmed."

"What about members of the basketball team from Boston Ferris being involved?"

"You tell me."

She noticed Marcus. Smiled prettily. "Are you from Boston Ferris?"

"You got it half right," McCain said. "He's from Boston. Excuse me."

Finally spotting an empty car, McCain dragged Marcus over, flashed his gold shield, asked the uniform there if he could borrow the backseat. Liz Mantell dogged his ass, a video cameraman picking up her valiant attempt to get the Big Story.

"Are you on the basketball team?"

McCain didn't let Marcus answer. He opened the back door to the cruiser, lowered the boy's head, and pushed him inside.

"Is he a suspect, Detective?"

McCain didn't answer and slid in next to Marcus.

"A morgue van has just pulled up," Mantell persisted. "How many fatalities were there?"

McCain smiled and shut the door, almost taking off the reporter's fingers. The interior was as dark and icy as a crypt. He stretched over the seat, managed to switch on the ignition. Cold air spilled out of the vents. Within a minute the air turned tepid.

McCain turned to Marcus, who'd buried his face in his suede gloves. Finally, the boy looked up. "I'll tell you what I told Mama. Nothing. 'Cause I didn't see anything."

"You weren't with Julius?"

"No, I wasn't with Julius. He was upstairs being butt-wiped by some shoe company conglomerate."

"Isn't that against NCAA rules?"

"Not if he didn't take anything."

"You think he paid for his own drink?"

Marcus frowned. "That is not the bling the board is concerned about."

"But if someone reported him, Marcus, he could get into trouble, right?"

"Yeah, I guess. But who's gonna report him?"

"Someone from the opposition."

"No one from the opposition is going to report Julius for copping a couple of free drinks. You don't get rid of a guy that way. That's a chickenshit way."

"Killing him is better?"

Marcus rubbed his temples. "Of course not. It's horrible, it's . . . I'm sick to my stomach. I play ball so I don't have to deal with the bangers. I do my job and they leave me alone. They respect my game, man. I worked hard so they can respect my game. I can't believe . . . Mick, I just want to go home. Please let me go home. I need to sleep."

"Just do me a favor. Tell me your version of what went down."

Marcus's sigh was long and weary. "I was sitting near the dance floor. Just hanging, you know. Talking up this girl."

"A Ducaine girl?"

"No, she was a local girl. I think she went to BU. Julius was hanging, too—making play with the ladies. I don't know every girl that was hanging on him. There were lots of them, that much I could tell you. It pissed Pappy off. The girl attention wasn't the issue. It was the fact that Julius humiliated Ducaine when he came back after being slammed. He and Pappy got into words."

"Who's Pappy?"

"Pappy is Patrick Delveccio. Ducaine's power forward."

"Was he the one that took Julius down on the court?"

"No, that was Mustafa Duran. He plays off the bench. He's known as the enforcer—for playing rough. Hey, no big deal. That's his job. But what happened last game went *way* beyond."

"What was he doing when Julius and Pappy got into words?"

"Mustafa wasn't at the club. He knew what would happen if he showed his face."

McCain stopped himself from pulling out his notebook. "What would happen?"

"Man, you can't do something like that on court without consequences."

"What kind of consequences?"

Marcus frowned. "C'mon, Micky. You know what it's like. If you don't defend yourself out there, you get slammed. Guys'll try all sorts of shit on you 'cause they think they can get away with it."

"So what kind of consequences are we talking about?"

"Not a gun, if that's what you think. I'm talking about on-court payback. You throw out an elbow when the refs aren't looking. And even if they are looking, after a dirty foul like that . . . hey, no one's gonna say anything."

"But we're not talking on court, Marcus. We're talking here. What do you think Julius would have done if Mustafa had showed up?"

"Well, he didn't show up, so the whole thing's conjecture."

"Who started the fight, Marcus?"

"No fight." The kid looked up. "Just a few words."

"What kind of words?"

"Julius was talking trash, okay? And Pappy was talking trash back. But there were lots more of us than there was of them. Things got a little heated. I think there was some pushing, but that's it. Ducaine left. Then Julius took a couple of girls upstairs, and that was the last I saw of him."

"What he do once he got the girls upstairs?"

Marcus looked puzzled. "Are you asking me if he did them at the club? That, I couldn't tell you. As far as I know, they were just arm candy, so he could look good to the corporates."

McCain took out his notebook. "You know the names of the girls?"

Marcus thought a moment. "No, not really."

McCain waited.

"I think I heard someone call one of the girls Spring. They were tall—the girls. One was about my height. I think they might be ballplayers, but not from Boston Ferris. I know all the girls from Boston Ferris."

"Who else went upstairs with Julius?"

"No one I knew."

"A bodyguard, maybe?"

"Nah, no bodyguard. Who'd mess with Julius?"

"He wasn't worried about fans getting too wild?"

"Julius wasn't that big yet. He was headed for the NBA, sure, but a Final Four title would have really been a sweet deal for him. He really wanted this title before he declared eligibility." Marcus shook his head. "This sucks! What a waste!"

"So what happened after he went upstairs?"

"I don't know what Julius was doing. I do know that Pappy came back with a couple of his banger buddies."

"About how much time had passed between Pappy's departure and Pappy's return?"

Marcus exhaled. "Maybe about a half hour, maybe a little longer. I wasn't watching the clock. When Pappy came back, everyone knew it was gonna be bad. I was coming out of the john, and when I saw him, I was already thinking about making my exit. Then the shooting started. I hit the floor. I didn't see no gun. I couldn't even tell you if Pappy was packing. I just heard the pop and dived for cover."

"So the words that Pappy and Julius had weren't over a girl?"

"Nah, it was the game, man. It's always the game. You cheated, you held me, you pushed me, you threw me an elbow, blah, blah, blah. It wasn't anything about a girl."

"Maybe Julius put the move on the wrong lady."

"No, I don't see that. He had his pick—anyone, any-time."

"Some guys get a thrill sticking it into other guys' girls."

"Nah, not Julius. His only passion was ball. Girls were just something to do when he wasn't playing ball. If he was going to square off with some guy seriously, it wouldn't be over a girl."

"So where did that rumor come from?"

"How should I know? If I was to guess, I'd blame Ducaine. Something to justify their actions. Everyone said that Pappy and his buds just gunned him down, Micky. Just mowed him down."

"But you didn't see it."

"That didn't mean it didn't go down that way." Marcus looked at McCain. "Who else would have shot him up?"

"So you're telling me that Van Beest hadn't pissed off anyone else but Ducaine?"

"No, Julius pissed off lots of people. *I* didn't like him. But I can't think of anyone who would have hated him enough to shoot him."

"Maybe you're not thinking hard enough."

"Maybe I need some sleep!" Marcus snapped back. "Maybe if I had some sleep, I could think better." He paused, then threw his head back. "I'm so cold. I'm so tired." He stared at McCain. "How do you guys do all-night stakeouts in this kind of weather?"

"We get cold and tired, too."

"So have a little sympathy, Micky. Let me go home."

McCain nodded. "I'll have a uniform drive you home."

"Don't bother. I'll hitch a ride with a friend."

"No, son," McCain told him. "An officer will take you home. Your mother wouldn't have it any other way."

8

Back Bay was landfill heaped into a dredged, stagnant bog, hence the name of its most famous landmark, Fenway Park. During the Victorian era, the bay had boasted some of the most fashionable houses in Boston. Scenic and charming, with cobblestone sidewalks and the breezes coming off the ocean, it was a heavily trod tourist spot during the warmer months. Throw in the ballpark and the clubs, and the area was a constant blur of action, as was most of D-4—the police district that patrolled it. McCain and Dorothy's home base.

At five in the morning, the shifts were changing. Detective Cory Wilde could have used a tag team, but it didn't work that way. Breton and McCain were picking up a good deal of the scut work, so he had little reason to bitch, but he'd been up for over twenty hours and it was getting to him. He suspected that Pappy Delveccio knew it, because the bastard wasn't giving him a damn thing. When he offered the kid a smoke, Pappy shook his head vehemently.

"I don't take that shit in my lungs. What you trying to do, man? Poison me?"

If only . . .

Wilde said, "Just trying to make you comfortable. You need a refill on water?"

Pappy leaned forward and glared. "I need to get outta here. Book me or let me go home, man."

The kid was six-ten, two eighty. From the waist down, Patrick Luther Delveccio looked like a beanpole. That was the way it was for basketball players—skinny, long legs meant for running and jumping.

From the waist up, it was a different story. The Ducaine star forward was carrying a heap of muscle around the arms and shoulders. His face was long and dark with fine features—almost Ethiopian.

Delveccio. Had to be part Italian. Or not. Look at Shaquille O'Neal and Tracy McGrady. Wilde was sixty percent Irish, had once thought the world was a simple place.

He faced Pappy again. Fancy boy, the hair all zigzagged in an intricate pattern, cornrows or whatever dripping down the nape of a long, muscled neck. Delveccio's brow was thick, his eyes were dark slits, and his lips were curled in a sneer.

Wilde tried not to sneer back. "You can speed it up by telling me the truth, Pappy."

The slits grew feral. "Have you been listenin', man? I am telling you the truth." His hands were inked with tattoos. Barely visible against the dark skin. Why bother?

Probably his arms, too, but Wilde couldn't see that. Pappy was wearing a long-sleeved white shirt. He'd taken off his olive-green silk suit jacket. It hung over his chair, smooth and gleaming. So long it puddled on the floor.

"I've been listening." Wilde shrugged. "But I don't

believe you. You know why I don't believe you? Because you're not credible."

"I didn't shoot no one." Delveccio crossed his arms over his chest.

"See, there you go again with that truth problem. We tested your hands for gunpowder residue, Pappy. You fired a gun."

"I didn't shoot no one at the club," he amended. "I was fooling around with a gun yesterday."

It was all Wilde could do not to snort. "When yesterday?"

"In the morning."

"And you haven't washed your hands since you fired that gun?"

"Matter of fact, I didn't."

"Haven't wiped your hands with a napkin after you've eaten?"

"No."

Wilde stared at him.

The kid retorted, "I'm a neat eater."

"You know, Pappy, last night's game was televised. All that sweat on your face and hands, just dripping and dripping and dripping. Not only did I see you wiping down your face and hands with a towel about twenty times, so did everyone who was watching the game. You want to change your story?"

"I want a lawyer."

"You lawyer up, Pap, but then I can't work with you. Then we can't work out a deal. And you know if you're gonna get out of this, you're gonna have to work up a deal."

Dorothy was watching from the other side of the interview room's one-way mirror. She looked at D-4's night captain. Phil O'Toole was beefy, florid, and white-haired, a third-generation Basic Irish Cop. He'd seen lots of changes in Back Bay: more immigrants, more drugs, more transients, and a lot more students. That meant more parties and more alcohol-related incidents. The upside was professionals coming back, fixing up old Victorian homes. No perps, those, just occasional victims.

"A Ducaine lawyer will be here any minute," she said. "How long do you think we can stall before the lawyer starts making demands to see the client?"

"We can put it off for ten minutes at the most," O'Toole replied. "What do we got on Delveccio—specifically?"

"Witnesses that saw him pull out a gun."

"How many witnesses?"

"Three or four and we're still looking."

"What else?"

"Residue on his hands. He obviously discharged a weapon, and it had to have been after the game."

"But you don't have anyone who *saw* him fire, right?"

"We're still looking," Dorothy repeated. "It's hard to get witnesses to talk."

"So you'll work on them."

"Of course."

O'Toole said, "Discharging a weapon . . . We have enough to keep him locked up until someone schedules an arraignment and makes bail. What's that? Three hours?"

"About."

They both regarded Wilde through the window. The detective rubbed his eyes and said, "Tell me about the shooting, Pappy. Tell me what happened. If it was self-defense, I want to know about it. The DA will want to know about it. Self-defense is a whole different thing."

The forward stared at Wilde, appearing to weigh his options. Then he said, "Your eyes are two different colors. What happen? Your mama bang two men at the same time?"

Wilde smiled. "I'll ask her the next time I see her."

"I've had enough." O'Toole picked up the phone and called Wilde out of the interview room. As soon as Wilde emerged, he started to defend himself. But O'Toole interrupted. "He asked for his lawyer, Cory. We're gonna have to book him based on what we have: witnesses to the fight, witnesses who saw him pullin' out a weapon, the residue on his hands."

"Give me a few more minutes with him," Wilde pleaded.

O'Toole's pink face turned the color of rare steak. "You deaf, Detective? He already asked for his lawyer. And some suit from Ducaine is on the way."

"So I'll tell him that. I'll tell him he don't have to talk to me. But let me keep him company, okay?"

O'Toole didn't answer.

"Just company," said Wilde. "Nothing that'll fuck up Miranda." He crossed himself.

"Fine," said O'Toole. "Company. Just until the suit gets here."

At that moment, McCain walked into the room. The captain stared at him. "Where have you been?"

"Talking to witnesses."

"And?"

"After much cajoling and threatening, I got two young ladies to admit they saw Pappy pull out and discharge a weapon—a handgun."

"Hallelujah!" Wilde said.

O'Toole said, "How reliable are they?"

"As reliable as anyone at the club. Which means they're shaky right now. We're gonna have to babysit them for a while."

"Did either one see Pappy point the gun in Julius's direction?"

"We're still nailing down the details."

"Anyone see what kind of gun Pappy fired?"

"No, sir, no one was paying that close attention. Too many people panicking when the bullets started flying. Everyone hit the floor." McCain consulted his notes. "I've also got a lead on a woman who was possibly with Julius on the upper level when he was shot. Her name is Spring Mathers, and she lives with her parents in Roxbury." McCain checked his watch. "It's a little after five. I figure I'll go over there in a few hours."

"No, you'll go over there now and wake them up," O'Toole said. "We need all the help we can get because our bad boy isn't saying much."

The door to the interview room opened. Officer Rias Adajinian was young and cute except for the dark circles under her eyes. A newcomer, she had been assigned the graveyard shift. It didn't agree with her biorhythm. "Someone from Ducaine University has arrived, demanding to speak with Mr. Delveccio. Also . . ." She sighed. "Ellen Van Beest is here, too."

O'Toole looked at Dorothy. Immediately, she said, "I know her. I'll do it." She looked at the young officer. "Where'd you set her up?"

"Five."

"I'll need a full pitcher of water, two glasses, and a big box of tissues." Dorothy paused. "Make that two boxes of tissues. Tell her I'll be there in just a second. I need a moment to myself."

"How did this happen?" Ellen grabbed Dorothy's arm, squeezing her fingers until her knuckles blanched. She was shaking, her voice wet with tears and profound sadness. "How did this happen? How could . . ." She broke into sobs that would no longer allow speech.

Tears in her own eyes, Dorothy reached out to embrace her, and the distraught woman permitted herself to take comfort. Like Dorothy, Ellen was a large woman—tall and heavy—but in grief, she was insubstantial.

"How could this happen? How could this happen? How could it, Dorothy, how could it?"

Water overflowed Dorothy's eyes. "We're going to find out everything, Ellen. I promise you, personally, I will not rest until we have the perpetrator behind bars."

"Just tell me this: Was it the pig who fouled my Julius? Did he take him down?"

"From what I heard, that boy wasn't even at the club."

"Boy." Ellen looked ready to spit. "It wasn't anyone from Ducaine?"

At Dorothy's silence, Ellen became fierce. "It wasn't him, it was his friend, wasn't it? *Wasn't* it? A Ducaine pig. Tell me the truth, Dorothy. Tell me! *Tell me!*"

"There were some players from Ducaine—"

"I knew it!" Ellen broke away. "I knew it! I knew it! The *game*! It's not a game when they allow monsters and thugs to play. This world's insane!" She was shouting now. "Insane!"

"I agree, but we don't know everything just—"

"I know enough to know it's insane!"

There was a knock at the door. Rias Adajinian came in. "Leo Van Beest is here."

Ellen pulled up a tissue and wiped her eyes. "Lord, this is all I need."

"You want me to put him in another room, Ellen?"

"Yes . . . no. No, he can come in." She faced Rias. "Bring him in here."

As soon as Adajinian left, Ellen started to pace. "We divorced when Julius was five. It was hard on the boy because Leo was still playing overseas. Not that Julius would have seen much of his father even if we had lived in Italy. With all his running around."

Her face had turned stony.

"It was hard on Julius after we both remarried. I don't think he ever forgave either one of us. He refused to take my husband's last name even after Paul adopted him. That's why I kept the name Van Beest. I wanted Julius to feel that connection . . . that we still belonged to each other. 'Cause Leo was never around."

She swallowed hard and continued to walk off her nervous energy by circling around the room like a herding dog.

"Never around, never paid for a damn thing. Spending on Lord knows what. Certainly not on his kid. Not only Julius, not on his other kids, either. Not that Leo was a bad man. He just wasn't a good man. He was just a regular man."

Ellen bit her thumbnail.

"The last time Leo divorced, it hit him hard. Real hard. He was fat and old and full of pain. His feet were gone, his knees were gone, his back was gone. Couldn't play ball and hardly any money left. Not that he was destitute. He's got his house, but it wasn't like his glory days, you know. The drinking started getting real heavy. I almost felt sorry for him. Julius . . . he did feel sorry for him. He made it a point to call him once a week, once every other week. Something like that. They got closer than they ever got."

"That was nice," said Dorothy.

"Yeah, it was nice. Julius was trying to reconnect. I think he was the only bright spot in Leo's dreary life. And now that's gone . . . Oh Lord, I need to sit down."

Dorothy helped her into a chair. "When was the last time you spoke to Leo?"

"Tonight at the game, actually." Ellen laughed bitterly. "We nodded to each other. That's what we did when we saw each other. We'd nod, all polite."

The door swung open, and Leo Van Beest barreled across the threshold. "Ellen!" He spread out his arms, but she was too weak to stand up. Instead, she just sobbed into her hands. He placed his own big mitts on her heaving shoulders. Tears were trailing down his cheeks. "Oh my, oh my, oh my!"

Leo had never been as tall as his son, had never had quite the athletic prowess. He'd played two seasons in the NBA before being cut, spent the next fifteen years overseas, always hoping to have that one magic season that would make the scouts back home stand up and take notice again. In his young years, at six-seven, he'd been as versatile at shooting guard as at small forward. But time had not been kind to him. He was now rotund, leathery, and gray. Looked like an oversize medicine ball. Sweat beaded his brow. He pulled out a handkerchief and dried off his face.

"How'd this happen?" he demanded of Dorothy.

"We're still investigating—"

"I don't want bullshit! I want answers!"

"And I will be happy to give them to you as soon as I know something."

"That's bullshit!"

Dorothy started to speak but thought better of it.

"What motherfucker shot my son?"

"We're still sorting out the details."

"I want that motherfucker strung up by his neck, you understand what I'm saying?"

"Yes, sir, I do."

"And if you people ain't gonna do it, I know people who will."

"Sir, the police are in control. We will find the perpetrator, I promise you."

"Yeah, I know what a promise from the police is worth."

Again, Dorothy didn't reply.

Leo's lower lip trembled. "Where is he? My son!"

"Oh Lord." Ellen started to cry. "I can't look at him like that, Leo. I just can't do it!"

"I know, Ellen. I'll do whatever needs to be done. You don't have to do it. I'll do it." He faced Dorothy. "I want to see him!"

"I'll see what I can arrange."

"Yeah, you go do that!" Leo ordered. "You *arrange* it right away, Detective. Right now! 'Cause Julius don't belong here at a police station. You understand? My son don't belong here." He started to cry. "He don't belong here!"

Helpless, Dorothy watched their pain and misery, making her problems appear very small. "Can I call someone for either of you? A minister maybe?"

"Pastor Ewing," Ellen said.

"Church of the Faith," Leo added. "He can help with . . . with what needs help with."

"He can make the arrangements." Ellen wiped off her face. In a clear voice, she announced to her husband that she'd accompany him to the morgue.

"You don't have to do it, Ellen," Leo said. "You don't have to."

"I know, but I'll do it anyway." She stood up, swayed a moment, but then regained her balance. "We brought him into the world together. We should say good-bye together."

9

"Well, that was a total bust!"

Even over her crackling cell, Dorothy heard the frustration in her partner's voice. "Spring Mathers wasn't home?"

"She never made it home," McCain said. "And I had to be the one to tell her parents about the shooting in the club. They hadn't a clue. They thought she was asleep, all tucked in cozy and warm. They charged into her bedroom, and when they found her bed still made up, they freaked. Started calling everyone they could think of to find out where she was."

"Oh boy."

"Yeah, oh boy!" McCain griped. "So instead of finding the one witness who may have been with Julius when he was shot, we now got a pair of hysterical parents who are filing a missing-person report and demanding answers. I'll tell you, Dorothy, this one's gonna bite the town in the ass. College is our tourist trade. Parents get too scared to send their kids here, we're in trouble. I'm not talking about Harvard or MIT. Cambridge is its own fiefdom. BU is an institution, sure. But what about all the Boston schools that feed off those babies?"

He was working himself up. Dorothy tried to keep her voice even. "I know. Sometimes it would be nice if things just went right."

There was a pause. McCain said, "I shouldn't be bitching. Your morning wasn't exactly coffee and the paper in bed. How'd it go with Ellen Van Beest?"

"As expected. The father was there, too. Leo. He played pro for a couple of seasons, although I don't remember him."

"Me, either. Jeez, I'm sorry. Must have been tough for you."

Images of despair crept into Dorothy's brain, of parents' faces when the doc on the monitor took off the sheet. Luckily she was able to convince them to do it via camera. Seeing the body in person would have been just too much.

Dorothy shuddered. "I'm going to bed, Micky. I told Doc C. to wake me up when he's done with the autopsy. I figure we'll go down for the briefing."

"C.'s doing the cutting himself, huh?"

Dorothy winced at his words. It made a difference, knowing the dead boy and his mother. The whole thing was nauseating. She was working hard to maintain her professionalism.

"You know what it's like," she said. "Big-time case. So what's on your schedule?"

"Sleep sounds good. Who do you think put the squeeze on, the mayor or all the way up to the governor?"

"Maybe both. It happened in Boston proper, but the governor has good reason to sweep it under the rug because both colleges are in Massachusetts." Dorothy shifted her cell from one ear to the other. "Either way, politics is going to take over. We'll get our asses whipped if we don't get a cut-and-dried solve."

"Any luck finding the matching weapon?"

"Techs are still going through the confiscated firearms. If we find the right gun, maybe Pappy left a usable print behind. He wasn't gloved when he discharged the gun. We know that from the powder marks."

"Except most prints are smeared by the kick of the recoil."

"Then maybe a palm print."

"Speaking of the son of a bitch, what's going on with Pappy?"

"He ain't a rich boy, but someone posted bail for him."

"Bail on murder?"

"Discharging a firearm's all it is so far."

McCain cursed. "Politics. Isn't it against NCAA rules for him to take gifts? Isn't bail a gift?"

"I doubt that's in the rule book, Micky. And Pappy has more important things to deal with than the NCAA board."

"Scumbag. We both know damn well that he was the shooter, even if he didn't mean to hit Julius. Let's just hope we can keep a good case against him. You know witnesses. Their memory gets foggy after the panic wears off. Even without politics, we gotta hope to get this nailed down in a couple of days or else things will start to get very murky."

"Look how long it took them to arrest that kid from Baylor . . . What was his name?"

"Carlton Dotson," McCain said. "Yeah, I forgot about that. What's with these basketball players anyhow?"

The question was rhetorical. Dorothy ignored it. "What was it? Six months before they issued the warrant?"

"Difference was Dotson confessed to one of his friends that he shot the other kid—Dennehy. And it took a while because there was no body. We sure have a body, but maybe I'd trade it for a confession."

Suddenly, Dorothy felt the crushing fatigue from the last twelve hours. "It's a waste of time talking about it. Try to get some rest, Micky."

"I'll try," McCain answered. "If I don't succeed, there's always drugs."

Dorothy expected to find both boys gone, had hoped to unwind by having her tiny house to herself. Instead, they were home, their faces grave and filled with what could have been remorse for every sin they'd committed in their lifetime. Seeing a "hero" gunned down could do that to you.

Big-time remorse: They'd prepared breakfast for her: toast and jam, coffee, fresh-squeezed orange juice. Upon seeing her, Marcus marked his place in his anthropology text, and Spencer looked up from his algebra homework. They regarded their mother; she looked back at them. Dorothy spoke first.

"Don't you boys have school?"

Marcus said, "Classes were canceled for the day."

"What's going on with the team?"

The older boy sighed and shrugged. "Everything's on

hold. We've got a meeting—the whole team's got a meeting—at three."

Dorothy looked at her younger son. "And you? What's your excuse?"

Spencer bit his lip. "I'm way behind, Mama. I'm trying to catch up, so I figured—"

"You can catch up on your own time, young man. Get packing."

"If you want, Mama, you can tell the school I have an unexcused absence. I can't go back to class until I know what's going on in algebra. It'll be wasting my time and I won't learn nothing. It'd be better if I studied here, but if you kick me out, I'll just go to the library or something."

Dorothy blew out air. "How long will it take you to catch up?"

"If I be working all day, maybe two days."

"You bet sweet Jesus you'll be working all day. Especially if I write you an excuse! No doing anything with your friends until you're all caught up." Spencer nodded and Dorothy sat down. "Thank you, boys, for making me some breakfast. I know that you're both doing it because you are feeling real bad about Julius. And you're feeling bad that I'm dealing with it . . . with his parents."

"That must have been awful," Spencer said.

Tears formed in Dorothy's eyes. "No words for it." She picked up a piece of toast and bit into it absently. "One of you guys pour me coffee." She sipped her juice. "Did you make decaf or regular?"

"Decaf," Marcus said. "Figured you might want to sleep."

"Good thinking," she said.

"Yeah, he's the smart one," Spencer said.

"Cut it out," Marcus retorted.

"Don't fight," Dorothy said.

"No one's fighting," Spencer said. "Can I talk to you for a moment?"

"I thought we were talking," Dorothy said.

Spencer said nothing.

"Go on," his mother urged.

"Maybe it's not the right time—"

"Go on!" Dorothy said testily.

Spencer cleared his throat and looked at his older brother.

Marcus put down a cup of coffee for his mother. "I'll be in the other room if you want."

"No, stay here," Spencer said. "I might need help."

Dorothy's eyes narrowed. "What'd you do this time?"

"I didn't do nothing. Just listen, okay?"

And then it dawned on her why she was snapping at him. Because it made her feel like a normal parent. At this moment, if she didn't act like a normal parent, she'd break down and sob, thanking the good Lord for her two beautiful sons and for keeping them healthy. She didn't want to do that—to be weak and vulnerable and helpless—in front of the boys.

She said, "I'm listening, but you ain't talking."

Spencer frowned. "All right. I'm gonna work real hard in school, Mama. I'm gonna . . . I'm gonna try not to get distracted by all the stuff that goes down there—the guns, the drugs, the gangstas. Lots of shit goes down there."

"Watch your mouth!"

"Sorry."

"No more carrying guns, right?"

"Yeah, right," Spencer said. "Can you let me finish?"

"Who's stopping you?"

Spencer didn't bother answering the obvious. "I'm gonna try real hard. But you have to know this. I know Marcus knows this. And I know I know this."

"Know what?"

"I'm getting to that, okay?"

No one spoke.

Spencer sighed. "Mama, I ain't a student. I don't like school, I don't like books, and I don't like keeping my ass parked for five hours when nothing goes on except people yawning, throwing things at each other, or even worse."

"There are some good teachers."

"They try, Mama, but it's a zoo. The classes are crowded, the books are old and boring, and I'm not interested in what they're teaching me." He looked desperately at his brother.

Marcus shrugged. "School's not for everyone."

"You shut up," Dorothy said. "Now, you listen here, young man—"

"Mama, please!"

Dorothy started to speak but stopped herself.

"Can I *finish*?" Spencer whined. When there was no comment from the big lady, he said, "I don't like dodging knives and bullets and drugs and people asking you to prove yourself or showing off their shit. I know, I know. My mouth. But that's what I deal with day in and day out."

"And what do you think I deal with?"

"The same thing. Which is why I came to this conclusion. If I'm gonna deal with the stuff—see, I said *stuff*—I might as well get paid for it. I don't want to go to no college. I don't have a college brain like Marcus does. Wait, Mama, don't interrupt."

"I didn't say nothing."

"It's on your face."

"Sure is," Marcus muttered.

"Didn't I tell you to shut it?" said Dorothy.

"Yes, Queen Dorothy, I apologize for my untimely interruption."

Despite herself, she smiled.

Spencer bit a nail and said, "Ma, I want to go to the academy. That's what I want to do if I don't make it in the pros."

Dorothy stared at her younger son. "The *police* academy?"

"No, *Exeter.*"

"Don't be fresh."

"Yeah, the police academy. I wanna be a cop if I don't make it in b-ball."

No one spoke. Finally, Marcus said, "Your coffee's getting cold, Ma."

"I don't care about my coffee."

"Don't yell," Spencer said.

"I'm not yelling, I'm talking with excitement! Spencer Martin Breton, I don't want you being a cop. You're too good for that."

Spencer looked down at the table. His lips quivered.

"What?" she demanded.

"Nothing."

"What?"

He kept his eyes averted. "I'm proud of what you do. Maybe one day, you'll be proud of yourself, Mama."

She had no answer for that.

"It's not my first choice," Spencer went on. "My first choice is playing pro ball. If I don't make it into the NBA,

I'll go to Europe. I know even that's a dream. And that's why I have a backup plan. Still, I believe in myself. I really do. Our high school made it to the semis. I think I can bring them to the finals. My coach thinks I can bring them to the finals. He believes in me, too."

"He's right," Marcus said.

"I believe in you, too, Spencer," Dorothy said. "Because you are that good. Which is why you can get an athletic scholarship."

"It's a waste of time and money, Mama. Let 'em give it to a kid that has a head for school. 'Cause I don't. I hate it!"

"Everyone needs a college education these days."

"No, Mama, everyone don't need a college education. But everyone needs a plan and I got a good plan. And I want you to support me on this."

Dorothy was silent.

"Or . . ." Spencer cleared his throat again. "Or if you can't support me right now, at least think about it."

"That seems fair," Marcus said.

Dorothy glared at him. To Spencer she said, "You don't know what you're getting into. Being a cop is very serious stuff. It's hard, it's stressful, it's long hours, and it isn't the least bit glamorous."

"I think I know what it is, Mama. This isn't something that just popped into my head. I been thinkin' about this for a long time. And that's all I have to say. Now, if you excuse me, I got studying to do."

The boy picked up his pencil and started doing some computations.

Marcus and Dorothy exchanged looks. The young man shrugged, sat back down, and picked up his text.

So now Spence wanted to be a cop: her son's flavor of the month. Teens changed their minds as often as they changed their socks. But the shooting did seem to add a new sobriety to Spencer's demeanor. He had a plan. He seemed motivated. He spoke passionately and assuredly. Maybe it would last longer than three days, but Dorothy had her doubts.

10

Because Dorothy had seen the body riddled with bullet holes at the crime scene, watched it pulled out on its slab from the meat locker drawer, she had a visceral aversion to seeing the corpse yet again. Sliced and diced and reassembled—a human jigsaw puzzle.

This boy had been her son's age, his teammate. It hit way, way too damn close to home. She asked the pathologist to speak with Micky and her in his office rather than around the cold steel table.

John Change was a fifty-year-old Harvard-trained forensic pathologist, born and raised in Taiwan. When applying to school thirty-two years ago, he'd thought the odds for acceptance greater with an Anglo name. Hence the *e* added to his surname. A modification that formed the basis for Change's entire comedy repertoire: "Change is good. Look at me."

He was a Boston fixture, did well in the marathon, had maintained the same height and weight for twenty-five years. The only visible signs of aging were silver streaks threading his sleek black hair.

The ME lab and his office were located in the basement of the morgue on Albany, clean, frigid, windowless, filled with a harsh bright light the sun wouldn't deem worthy of reproduction. The office was a spacious room, but Change had stuffed it with books, notebooks, magazines, and jars of tissue preserved in formaldehyde. Most of the specimens were teratomas, which, Dorothy had learned, were bizarre tumors that stemmed from undifferentiated cells. Change's favorites contained hair, bone fragments, and teeth; if you looked at some of them in a certain light, they appeared to be grinning gargoyles. Standing amid the anomalies were snapshots of Change's pretty wife and two bright-eyed children.

Dorothy had been the last one to arrive, but Micky told her that he had gotten there only a few minutes before. He was looking worn around the seams; the kind of drawn expression that comes from lots of stress, very little sleep, and no resolution in sight. He sat in one of two chairs opposite Change's desk, drinking coffee out of a paper cup. She took it from him, sipped, made a face.

"This is awful."

"You didn't give me a chance to warn you. Sit down."

Dorothy debated whether to hang up her coat, then nixed the idea. The ambient temperature was worse than a frozen food aisle.

McCain said, "Delveccio was released a few hours ago."

"What was the bail?"

"Fifty thou."

"Who posted?"

"Ducaine, like we guessed."

"Where's the doc?" Dorothy asked.

"Change is changing." McCain smiled at his own wit.

"Actually, I'm here." Change stepped inside and shut the door. He was wearing a suit and tie, but his pant legs were rolled up and his feet were encased in rubber-soled work shoes. "My good shoes are upstairs. Lizard. It's a bitch to get the smell out. The leather absorbs the odors, and reptilian hides seem more porous, which is counter-intuitive, no? Not that I smell anything anymore, but my wife sure does. It's our anniversary tonight."

"Happy anniversary," McCain said.

"How many years?" Dorothy asked.

"Twenty-eight."

"Long time."

"Denise puts up with a lot," said Change. "Long hours and I'm a ghoul. Still, she knows where I am and that my profession doesn't lend itself to cheating." He sat down and placed his folded hands on the desktop. "I expected to find something routine. Instead, I found something interesting. Julius Van Beest bled to death but not from the gunshot wounds. By my estimation, none of them were fatal."

Change spread four Polaroids on his desktop. "These are the gunshot wounds: two that coalesced into each other and skimmed the right temple region, the two holes in the arm, and one through the shoulder. The last one had the highest probability of being fatal until I saw that the bullet went through muscle only."

He laid out two more Polaroids, both of them gruesome. Dorothy drew her head back.

McCain screwed his lips up in disgust. "What're we looking at, Doc?"

"The interior of Mr. Van Beest's thoracic cage. This is

what I saw when I opened him up. There's nothing discernible anatomically because the entire region is swimming in blood." Change looked up from the photographs. "After I cleaned up the area, I can say with authority that the boy died of a burst in the subclavian artery where it comes off the arch of the aorta. And by my estimation, the cause of the burst was an aneurysm, which is a fancy word for a weakness in the vessel wall. Because the wall is weak, it eventually forms an out-pouching—a sac, if you will. It's like a balloon. And you know what happens when the balloon inflates. The walls get thinner and thinner until you blow too much air in and, bingo, it pops."

The detectives were speechless. Finally, McCain said, "How'd that happen? The aneurysm?"

"Usually, it's a preexisting condition. But I could postulate that the paramedics may have inadvertently brought about a vascular accident as they attempted CPR. A real Greek tragedy, when you think about it."

Dorothy couldn't draw words from her throat.

"From your point of view," Change went on, "you need to keep in mind that you may not be able to charge your suspect with premeditated murder. Only attempted murder, because the gunshot wounds weren't the direct cause of death."

"But"—Dorothy cleared her throat—"why would the paramedics do CPR unless his heart had stopped?"

McCain picked up on her question. "There you go: Shock from being shot stopped his heart in the first place. So you could give us a direct link to Delveccio, right, Doc?"

"His heart *had* to have stopped," Dorothy insisted.

"It's a thought," Change admitted. "Even so, the defense could argue that the gunshot wounds combined

with a preexisting arterial defect might have been enough
for a precipitous drop in blood pressure. He could've had
a pulse, but a very faint one, and the EMTs missed it."

"But still, there's a direct link to the gunshot wounds."

"Unfortunately, Detective Breton, that's all theory. In
a medicolegal context, the gunshot was not the cause of
death. Mr. Van Beest expired due to a burst artery. And
we have no way of knowing precisely when that occurred.
The defense could even argue that the paramedics made
it worse, that without their compressions the victim
would've survived. Each downward motion against the
sternum could have caused the wall to stretch wider and
wider until it ripped open. The area is right below the
clavicle near where the aorta splits into the carotid artery
that feeds the head and the subclavian artery that feeds
the upper body. These are major vessels that transport
lots of blood."

"That's ridiculous," said McCain.

"Perhaps, but it's more than reasonable doubt."

The room fell silent.

McCain cleared his throat. "The stress of getting shot
had to make his heart beat faster, which would put stress
on that sac, right?"

Change didn't speak.

"Isn't that so, Doc?"

Change picked up a pencil and waved it like a wand.
"Yes, the sympathetic nervous system kicks in under stress.
I'm sure at some point his heart was beating very rapidly."

"So would that increase the likelihood of the
aneurysm tearing open?"

"That's more than speculative. I could surmise, but I
wouldn't know how fast his heart had been beating. The

defense would seize on that. If I were Delveccio's lawyer, I'd keep focusing on the compressions."

Dorothy said, "There is no way the burst artery could have been caused by one of the gunshot wounds?"

Change shook his head. "No hole was found in the area."

"What about a deflected bullet?"

"That's not what happened, Detective."

"Julius fell on his chest when he was shot," Dorothy said. "Maybe the thump on his chest burst open the aneurysm."

Change thought about that. "It's a possibility. But then again, I heard he got hit pretty bad across his chest at last night's game. The defense could argue that that was the triggering event."

"We were there," Dorothy said. "It looked to me like he got hit in the neck."

Change said, "A long arm fouling him like that probably impacted his neck, face, and chest. Must've been a severe blow to knock such a large man down. I hear he was out on the floor for quite a while."

"He came back and played the game of his life," Dorothy said.

"That doesn't mean damage wasn't done. Perhaps the fouling did exacerbate an arterial tear. Combine that with chest compressions . . ." Change threw up his hands.

McCain said, "Defense this, defense that. How about giving *us* something to work with?"

"I just want to tell you what you could be up against—what the DA will consider when you plead your case. On attempted murder, Detectives, you've got a cakewalk. But I couldn't say beyond a reasonable doubt that the aneurysm burst because of anything the shooter did."

"That's crazy," McCain said.

"Attempted murder is still jail time," Change said.

"It's not the same as premeditated murder," McCain said. "That would be life without parole, and that's what the asshole deserves—shooting up a club like that."

"Can I go back to something?" Dorothy said. "You said you thought it was a preexisting condition."

"Almost certainly. If it was an aneurysm."

"If?"

"Theoretically," said Change, "it could have been a stress tear. But I'd consider that highly unlikely, and I'd have to say so on the stand."

"Still," said Dorothy, "it's not impossible, right? And couldn't a stress tear have resulted from a bad fall onto the table after he got shot? Which would put us right back to the shooting as the main cause."

"I don't think a fall on the table would do it."

"But how about if it wasn't a preexisting condition?"

Change said, "But how would you know that unless you had prior X-rays of the region?"

Dorothy smiled. "At Boston Ferris, all athletes are required to have yearly checkups, including chest X-rays. I know that from my own baby. Since Julius was on the team going on his fourth year, that means four X-rays. This aneurysm, it would show up on a chest X-ray, right?"

Change nodded. "If it was large enough, yes."

"And the doctor seeing this . . . they certainly wouldn't have let him play with it, right?"

Again, Change nodded. "*If* it was big enough and *if* someone saw it. The artery runs behind the clavicle. The aneurysm could've been hidden by bone."

"But maybe it wasn't. And they let him play. And he played for four years with no problem."

Change shrugged.

"I think Dorothy's onto something," McCain joined in. "It's worth taking a look at the X-rays. 'Cause if it didn't show up, maybe it was hidden by bone, sure. But maybe it just wasn't ever there in the first place. Meaning that maybe falling on the table caused the artery to burst, Doc."

"Detective, arteries don't just explode."

"But you can't tell me what *did* happen at a hundred percent certainty, right?"

"I can tell you that a bullet hole didn't cause the artery to burst," Change said. "There was no puncture wound from any external cause. Nor were there any bone fragments that could have pushed through. Ergo, the cause has to be idiopathic—something internal, unique to Mr. Van Beest."

"See, Doc," McCain said, "I'm thinking that if no one saw anything on all the chest X-rays that Julius took for four years, this aneurysm musta been pretty tiny. Then maybe we can make a solid case for his heart going haywire during the shooting."

Dorothy said, "I still like the fall on the table. His blood pressure, like you said, nosedived and his heart stopped."

"Exactly," McCain said.

Dorothy moved closer to Change's desk. "He was a goner even before the paramedics got to him."

Change listened to their routine and smiled faintly. "I couldn't state any of that as definitive, Detectives."

"But you couldn't state that it *didn't* happen that way," said Dorothy. "And with nothing showing up on any X-ray . . ."

"First you've got to get the DA to buy it."

"You take care of the medical angle," McCain said. "We'll worry about the DA."

"I can't promise I'll be able to say what you want."

"Doc, you do your job and we'll do ours. I'm sick of letting these thugs get away with a slap on the wrist!"

"Attempted murder isn't a slap on the wrist," Change said.

"If we charge premeditated and it's pled down to attempted murder, I'll be okay with it," McCain said. "Otherwise you know what we got? We got attempted murder that'll be pled down to a misdemeanor discharging a firearm in a public place and inciting panic. Which carries jail time but not what this bastard deserves."

"That seems a bit pessimistic," Change said. "The victim *was* shot."

"And the bastard will say he didn't mean to shoot him, he was just horsing around, had a couple drinks too many. I know how it works with thugs, Doc. Especially athletic thugs. The lawyers stack the jury with fans. We need the maximum charge and work down from there."

Change sat back in his chair. "It's your call."

"Damn right!" McCain was working himself up.

Dorothy broke in. "If I get you a recent X-ray, Doc, you'll read it, right?"

"Of course," Change said. "Actually, now you've got me curious." He paused. "Getting an X-ray—that's clever."

"She's a clever woman," McCain said. "That's why they call her detective and you doctor."

11

The product of a merger between Boston Electronic and Technical and Ferris Fine Arts Academy, the college was a solution that had pleased both financially strapped institutions back in the fifties. Pooling dual resources, the new BF board bought a defunct prep school and modeled its hybrid after New York's Cooper Union: an Athenian meld of fine arts, practical arts, and science.

But with a twist. Boston Ferris had been chartered to serve the *town* portion of Boston's town and gown dichotomy. The college admissions committee went out of its way to select its own. The academy with a heart.

Athletics hadn't even been part of the curriculum until the board discovered that many locals, brought up in the streets, clocked beaucoup hours shooting hoops. Soon afterward, Boston Ferris began to actively solicit athletes, and its enrollment ballooned. The school built a state-of-the-art gymnasium, workout room, and pool and sauna and began offering sweetheart majors like Applied Electronics and Practical Waterway Services—a fancy name for plumbing. The subtle switchover didn't concern Micky McCain and Dorothy Breton. What did matter was that the college's Human Health Services hadn't been updated since the merger.

That was never as in never *ever*.

The place was a morass of bureaucracy rivaled only by the Boston Police Department, and like BPD, every request had to be made in writing. The dogmatic stupidity was driving McCain over a wall. Dorothy wasn't doing too much better.

"This is a homicide investigation," she said. "We can't get the patient's permission because he's dead!"

They were talking to Violet Smaltz, a sixty-three-year-old crone with a perpetual scowl and a face like a paper bag. She narrowed her eyes and snorted.

"I *know* the boy is dead, Detective. And it wouldn't make a difference if he were alive. If the medical examiner's office wants the medical records, then let the medical examiner's office put in a request of transfer for the medical records and send it in with the correct paperwork. Medical documents are transferred from physician to physician."

"This is bullshit!" McCain blurted.

Violet glared at him. "No need for foul language, Detective McCain."

"I could get a subpoena—"

"Then get one!" Violet folded her hands across her chest. She was wearing a long gray skirt and a gray cardigan sweater that hung on her bony frame. She looked like a faded scarecrow.

Dorothy gave up. "Well, could you at least get us the correct paperwork?"

Violet didn't budge. She continued to glare at McCain.

"Please?" Dorothy begged.

Another snort. "One minute."

As soon as she was gone, Dorothy said, "Getting nasty won't work, Micky."

"Yeah, it works. It works for me."

Smaltz came back a few minutes later. "There are three copies here. Be sure all three are filled out legibly."

McCain snatched the papers from Violet's grasp. "I bet I wouldn't have to go through this rigmarole if I was President McCallum."

"Well, you're not President McCallum, are you, now?"

Outside, Dorothy snaked her scarf around her neck. "Very smooth, Micky. As soon as she gets the request, she'll throw it in the circular file."

"Not her. That wouldn't be following accepted procedure. I wish there was some way to stick it to that bitch."

"She's probably the only one in Health Services who knows where everything is."

"Everyone has to die sometime."

"What am I gonna do with you?"

"You're gonna congratulate me," McCain said. "I gave myself an idea. As in President McCallum. How 'bout we go find him? Maybe he can streamline things."

"What makes you think he'll talk to us?"

"Well, we won't know unless we try."

Trying took forty-five minutes of badge flashing and passing from one security point to another. Finally, they were escorted up to a suite of penthouse offices atop the five-story Administration Center. President McCallum didn't have just a secretary, he had a staff. Dorothy counted at least fifteen cubicles, most of them manned by college kids. Probably work-study.

McCain was surprised by the size of the president's office—much smaller than he had expected. Still, it had all the amenities: glossy walnut-paneled walls, a well-stocked wet bar, carved bookshelves, and a gleaming rose-wood desk. And McCallum's own Christmas tree, high and green in a windowed corner. The view beyond was a New England winter picture postcard.

McCallum was a beefy man with white hair, a complexion more florid than a sea captain's, a veined potato nose, and watery blue eyes. His sagging face and rumpled suit suggested he hadn't had much sleep in the last twenty-four hours.

Join the club, McCain thought. He and Dorothy sat opposite the man, with the fancy desk between them. The room was hot as blazes. Dorothy was sweating because she still had her coat on. She took it off, and McCallum motioned to a hardwood hall tree where a black cashmere overcoat hung.

"How are you, Detectives?"

"I'm fine, sir," McCain answered.

"Well, I'm not," McCallum said. "It's been a horrible day, and I'm afraid I'm a bit off my mark. Make yourselves comfortable. I pride myself on being more in tune with working stiffs than with the nabobs of academia. I grew up in this city. My father was a dockworker and my mother slaved in the mills. I went to Boston Ferris myself."

"Local boy made good," McCain said.

Sarcasm in his voice, but McCallum missed or chose to ignore it. "I call it giving back to a community that believed in me."

"Good for you, sir," said McCain.

Dorothy kicked him in the shins.

McCallum said, "What can you tell me about the status of the investigation? Have you arrested that animal?"

"What animal?" McCain asked.

"You know as well as I know. The boy is a thug. He deserves to be behind bars for what he did."

"Who are you talking about?" McCain said.

"We're not trying to be . . . evasive," Dorothy said. "We just want to know if we're all on the same page."

"Like maybe you know something that we don't know?" Micky added.

McCallum's eyes turned hard. He folded his hands, set them on his shiny desktop, and leaned forward. "The school is in mourning over a terrible loss. As a matter of fact, the entire city is in crisis. Have you read the morning newspapers?"

"I'll go you one better," McCain said. "I talked to the stringers last night."

"Then you understand the mayhem I've been dealing with. I've been on the phone with Ellen Van Beest all morning, and in between I've been fielding calls from the chief of police, the mayor, and the governor. From what I understand, the legislature's preparing to order a special session investigating athletes and violence. That's especially irritating because it's all a *crock!*"

"Violence is a crock?" Dorothy asked.

"Of course not. But the canard linking sports to aggression, the nonsense about nightclubs being battlefields, is simply overblown rubbish! A tragedy occurs, and in typical fashion the media blow it way out of proportion. Then the officials start quaking, worrying that parents will stop sending their kids to Boston. All because of a once-in-a-blue-moon aberration."

"Once in a blue moon?" McCain asked.

"When was the last time you heard of an athlete shot at a club?"

"Paul Pierce getting knifed don't count?"

"That was five years ago," said McCallum. "Last I heard, the man recovered fully. He's an all-star, for God's sake. So let's not be diverted by yesterday's news." His jaw clenched. "My scheduling is very tight. Is there anything specific I can do for you?"

"As a matter of fact . . ." Dorothy handed McCallum the triplicate paperwork given to her by Violet Smaltz. "We need Julius Van Beest's medical records and would like you to facilitate that."

"What is this?" McCallum asked.

"Red tape," McCain said. "From your health center."

McCallum scanned the documents and made a face. "Why do you need Julius's medical records?"

"Just being thorough, sir," Dorothy said.

"Who wants to see them?" McCallum asked.

"The medical examiner."

"For what purpose?"

"Being thorough," Dorothy repeated.

McCallum shook his head. "It's not my call, Detective. If the ME wants to see the records, let him make a formal request. That's standard procedure."

"Yeah, we know that," McCain said. "But being as this is a homicide investigation and everyone is anxious for it to be settled up quickly, we were just wondering if you could help us out."

Dorothy said, "You know how it is, sir. The newspapers

are hungry for information, and we'd love to tell them Boston Ferris is cooperating thoroughly in every aspect of the investigation."

"We *are* cooperating thoroughly," said McCallum. "Put in the proper paperwork and you'll have the records."

Neither detective moved.

McCallum sighed disgustedly. "All right. All right. I'll make a phone call." He patted the paperwork. "Even though this *is not* appropriate procedure."

"Thank you very much, sir," Dorothy said. "We really appreciate it."

"It benefits everyone," McCain added.

"Yeah, yeah." McCallum picked up the phone. "You don't know what a favor I'm doing for you. To add to my current misery, I now have to deal with Violet Smaltz!"

12

In tune with working stiffs'!" McCain grumbled under his breath as he started the car. "What an asshole!"

Dorothy held aloft a manila envelope. It held Julius Van Beest's most recent X-ray taken for Boston Ferris. "He got us what we wanted."

"Y'know, if you're a snob, be honest and act like one." He turned the heater up full blast. "Then we'd all know what we were dealing with."

"This is Boston. You should be used to it by now," Dorothy said. "First it was the Brahmins. Now it's the universities. We serve and protect in the land of pretentious eggheads."

McCain's cell rang. He fished it from his pocket and flipped open the lid. "McCain . . . That's wonderful, Mrs. Mathers, just great. I'd like to— Yes . . . Yes . . . Yes . . . I understand, Mrs. Mathers, but she's a material witness— Yes . . . Yes, I see. Can we maybe come down and just talk to you for a few minutes? I promise you, we'll be discreet— Hello?" He blew out air. "She hung up on me."

"Who did?"

"Rayella Mathers. Her daughter, Spring, is alive and well and at an undisclosed location, quote unquote, calming down her nerves."

"Scared."

"Who wouldn't be scared of that thug?"

"Now, what thug are we talking about?" Dorothy kidded.

McCain smiled and thought a moment. "I need you to come with me to the Mathers house. You gotta convince the missus to let us know where Spring is."

"You want me to talk to her as one black woman to another."

"As one strong, brave black *mother* to another. How about we drop Julius's X-ray at the morgue and catch up with the doc later. We need to get to Spring before Pappy does."

Dorothy said, "He couldn't be that stup— Never mind. Let's go."

It didn't take too much prodding from Dorothy to convince Rayella Mathers to give them her daughter's "secret" whereabouts. Distant cousin's apartment in Roxbury, another shared-house situation.

But it took a great deal of prodding from Dorothy to convince Rayella not to warn her daughter that the police were coming. They didn't want the girl to bolt.

As soon as they got to the place, the detectives worked on their strategy. They were pretty damn sure that Spring wasn't going to open the door on her own, and neither one of them had the paperwork to order her to do so. After some discussion, they decided on Dorothy doing her best imitation of Rayella while standing just out of peephole range.

Spring Mathers opened the door, saw strangers, and shrank back in terror. She almost succeeded in slamming the door in their faces, but McCain was too quick with his shoulder. "Just a few minutes, Spring." He pushed his way inside and showed her his gold shield. "I swear we're here to make your life easier."

"Then get yo' funky ass the hell outta here! Get out! Get *out*!"

She was loud, but Dorothy was louder. "If we found you, girl, you think it's gonna be all that hard for Pappy to do the same? Now, you just calm yourself down and thank Jesus that we got here before he did!"

The words clicked in Spring's frightened brain. She took two steps backward, then folded her arms across her chest. No wonder Julius had his sights set on her. She was a knockout: creamy mocha skin, round wide eyes, luscious thick red lips, perfect cheekbones. Slim but busty with a perfect high-water booty. Even in Dorothy's thin days, she'd never had a figure like that.

"What do you want?" This time Spring's voice was a hoarse whisper.

"We want to put Pappy Delveccio behind bars. Isn't that what you want as well?"

"I didn't see no shots." Tears streamed down the girl's smooth cheeks. "That's the truth, lady. I didn't see no shots, and I didn't see no one shoot." She was crying now. "Why can't you leave me alone?"

"'Cause we don't want the animal who shot Julius to walk," McCain said.

"Who you think he's gonna come after if he don't get put away?" Dorothy asked her.

"Not if I don't say nothin'!" Spring retorted. "And there's nothin' to say 'cause I didn't see nothing. I just heard it. *Pop, pop, pop,* you know. That's it. I was too scared to look around and see who was shooting."

McCain took out his notebook. "Where were you sitting?"

"Next to Julius. He was like makin' his move, talking nothin' but sugar. I knew what was comin'." She shrugged. "It was fine with me."

"You're doing good, Spring," Dorothy said. "Now, where was Julius sitting?"

Spring regarded her with disdain. "At the table."

"Where at the table?"

"What do you mean?"

McCain said, "The tables were positioned by the railing, right?"

Spring nodded.

Dorothy said, "Was he looking over the railing, or did he have his back to the railing?"

Spring squinted as she attempted to retrieve the image from her memory bank. "He was sitting . . . looking over the railing . . . looking at the door so he could check out who was coming in. Then he said . . . he said, 'Uh-oh, Pappy's back.' He stood up. That's when I heard the popping. Everyone started screamin'."

She put her hands over her face. "I hit the ground, bundled myself up in a little ball, and started prayin' to Jesus." She dropped her hands and shook her head. "When it was over, Julius was lying across the table, blood coming outta him." She stared at Dorothy. "I never saw Pappy and I never saw him take out no gun."

Dorothy tried to slow it down. "Spring, when you got

up, you remember seeing Julius across the table. Was he on his stomach or on his back?"

"I think he was on his stomach. He fell with a big thump. I heard that. I remember thinking that he was gonna break the table and crush me to death."

"So he fell pretty hard," Dorothy said.

"Yeah," Spring said. "He fell hard. But I didn't see no one shoot him."

McCain said, "If you didn't see Pappy shoot, you didn't see him shoot. All you have to do, Spring, is tell us what you heard Julius say, then tell us what you saw."

"I ain't gonna say anything. I'm scared shitless of that animal."

"We can protect you—"

"That's bullshit! Police don't protect no one, specially not a black woman." Spring looked at Dorothy. "And you being here ain't gonna change any of that."

"We'll subpoena you, Spring," McCain said.

"First you gotta find me. The next time I won't make it so easy."

"We should arrest her," McCain said.

"On what grounds?" Dorothy took out her cell phone.

"Material witness to a murder, and she's a flight risk. Also, screaming at the cops."

"She didn't witness anything substantive," Dorothy said. "Once we got Pappy under lock and key, she'll calm down. Can you start the car and turn on the heat? I'm freezing. God, this must be the coldest December on record."

"That's what you say every year."

"Just start the car, please."

McCain complied, turning the heat to the max as Dorothy checked her phone messages. Within seconds the car smelled like scorched wool. "Anything important?"

"Captain O'Toole wants to talk to us."

"That ain't good."

"Probably not."

"He didn't say why?"

"Just his secretary telling you and me to come in at two."

"I don't like this."

"Shhh . . . " Dorothy concentrated as she listened to her voice mail. She pressed the disconnect button and flipped down the lid on her phone. "Dr. Change called. The X-ray didn't show any aneurysm."

"You're kidding!"

"No, I'm not."

"So that's good, right?" McCain said.

"Despite that, he's sure an aneurysm killed Julius."

"How can that be?"

"Could be like Change said. A bone blocked it on the X-ray."

"Or Julius died of a gunshot wound Change overlooked."

"Keep that to yourself when we meet with him, Micky." Dorothy checked her watch: 1:15. "We can't make it to the ME office and back before two. I'll tell Change we'll be there by three-thirty, maybe four o'clock."

"Sounds good."

"Maybe we should grab some lunch in the meantime," Dorothy said.

"Lunch." McCain laughed. "Now, there's a novel idea."

13

"Four sounds fine," Change told Dorothy over the line. "If I'm a little late, just wait for me."

"No problem, Doc. Can I ask you a few questions?"

"If they're about the X-ray, I'm not at the morgue now."

"Just your impressions."

"I know what you're going to ask. At a quick glance, I didn't see any radiographic evidence of an aneurysm. But that doesn't mean it wasn't there. I still say that that was the most likely cause of death."

"Okay, let's assume the aneurysm was there." Dorothy switched her cell from one ear to the other. "Might we assume that it was small?"

"Maybe."

"And if it was small—a little out-pouching that didn't even show up on the X-ray—and if Julius fell splat on the table, could we assume that an impact like that might have caused a tiny aneurysm to burst . . . theoretically?"

"Why don't we wait until we're at the morgue for this discussion?" Change said.

"Just answer me this. Could that have happened, that his falling caused the aneurysm to open up?"

"Anything's possible," Change said. "But you'll want stronger evidence than that going into court." A pause. "That's my opinion anyway."

"Thank you." Dorothy hung up and looked at McCain. "I'm in the mood for kosher pastrami—that Romanian stuff. We're two blocks away from Rubin's. Okay with you?"

"Sounds like a plan," said McCain. "What did Change say?"

"The fall's a maybe, maybe not. Not strong enough to go to court with—in his opinion."

"Opinions are like assholes," McCain said. "Everybody's got one."

Captain O'Toole closed the door to the interview room—a windowless, airless space with barely enough room for a standard-issue table and chairs. The floor was a mosaic of mismatched green granite tiles; the once sunshine-yellow walls were now a faded mustard. The captain pulled out a chair with his foot and sat backward, with his stomach pressed against the splats. He was flushed, forehead dotted with beads of sweat. He took a handkerchief from his pocket and gave his face a firm wipe.

With him was Harriet Gallway, who had put in ten years with the DA's office. She was very petite, so slight that people noticed her only because of her flaming-red hair. She had gobs of it, flying over her shoulders and trailing down her back. She wore a hunter-green suit and black flats. Her green eyes sparkled when she smiled. But she wasn't smiling now.

"Hot in here," she muttered.

"Don't smell too good, either," O'Toole added. "All of you have a seat."

Dorothy and McCain exchanged glances and sat down.

O'Toole nodded to Harriet. "Ladies first."

Harriet cleared her throat. "My boss tells me that Delveccio's counsel is running the story that Julius died from natural causes."

"Not exactly," McCain said.

"I don't like that," O'Toole said. "What does that mean, 'Not exactly'?"

"That's what we're trying to determine, sir."

"Who's we?" Harriet asked.

"Dr. Change," Dorothy said. "John Change. He thinks Julius died from an aneurysm and not from a gunshot wound."

"He *thinks*?" O'Toole said.

McCain muttered, "He thinks, therefore he screws us up."

"That's his conclusion so far," Dorothy said.

Harriet said, "Oh my."

"Still," Dorothy said, "Delveccio's gunshots could have caused the aneurysm to burst. Because when Julius was hit, he fell forward onto a table."

McCain said, "The force on his chest from slamming against the table could very well have burst open the aneurysm."

"So the shots lead to the chain of events that caused Julius Van Beest's death," Harriet said. "We still could make a case for premeditated murder."

"Is that what happened?" O'Toole said. "A fall killed him? Change says that?"

Dorothy said, "The fall didn't cause the aneurysm—if there *was* an aneurysm. But it could have caused an aneurysm to open up."

"What do you mean, if there *was* an aneurysm?"

"So far, nothing showed up on the X-ray," Dorothy said.

O'Toole said, "This is starting to stink like bullcrap."

Harriet played with her hair. "So it's possible he didn't have an aneurysm."

McCain said, "Change is sayin' right now that there's no physical evidence of one on the X-ray."

"So how did he come to his conclusion that Julius died of an aneurysm?"

"There was a ruptured artery upon autopsy and blood pooling in the chest cavity," said Dorothy. "I respect Change, but I'm wondering if maybe he missed a bullet wound."

"You're saying Change fucked up?" said O'Toole.

"No one's perfect," McCain half whispered.

As the captain colored further, Dorothy broke in: "We're meeting with him in an hour. We'll go over everything in detail."

"Cancel your meeting," O'Toole snapped. "We got more important things to deal with. As in, we found the gun that shot Julius in the pile of confiscated weapons. As in, on the damn thing was a partial of Delveccio's right thumb."

Dorothy and McCain smiled. She said, "You pick him up?"

"He's in holding as we speak. The bad news is that our witnesses who said they saw Pappy pulling out a gun have recanted. But with the print, we know the asshole touched the gun at some point. And we know that the same gun shot Julius."

"I think a jury can put two and two together," Dorothy said.

"But," Harriet said, "if I'm trying to prove premeditation, I have to make sure Julius was killed by the gun as part of an intentional, direct action committed by the accused. Now you're telling me we don't know that."

O'Toole glared at the detectives.

McCain said, "That's a question for Change. But in the meantime—"

"Here's the thing," said Harriet. "If we go for attempted murder rather than homicide, Pappy's counsel is going to know we can't prove the gun killed Julius. It's going to give him ammunition to fight even that charge."

"So what do you want from us?" Dorothy said.

"I want you to see if you can get him scared about premeditated murder," the DA said. "Then we can probably deal him down to attempted murder. Otherwise we could end up settling for some dinky charge."

"That's ridiculous!" McCain said. "He was aiming for Julius, he touched the damn gun, and the bullets hit their mark."

"But not necessarily fatally, Detective. And if we don't get someone who saw Pappy fire the gun, we end up with a break in the chain. And Pappy can be very charming when he wants to be," Harriet said. "Get some b-ball fans on the jury, maybe a swooning female or two, we could be in trouble."

The room fell silent.

McCain spoke first. "How about this: We don't have conclusive evidence of an aneurysm on the X-ray. So at this particular moment, I don't know what killed Julius. Meaning I can tell Delveccio it was his bullet." He shrugged. "Hell, Supreme Court says I'm allowed to deceive, right? Let me go in there now and work him."

"He's already asked for his lawyer," Harriet said. "When he was picked up the first time."

"I didn't hear him ask for his lawyer today."

"That's irrelevant," Harriet said. "Once he requests—"

"Unless he chooses of his own volition to talk to me," said McCain. "Coupla guys shooting the breeze."

O'Toole said, "Why in blazes would he do that?"

McCain smiled. "You know, Captain, when I want to be, I can be charming, too."

Through the one-way mirror, McCain looked at Patrick Luther Delveccio, a huge, broad-shouldered figure barely out of his teens. An indulged child in an oversize body, and that made him menacing. He was dressed casually—jeans and a sweatshirt. Musta been size 20 athletic shoes—fancy blue shoes—housed his feet. The kid's mouth was set petulantly, but his body was all move-ment: hands drumming the tabletop, feet tapping the floor, head bopping to an internal beat. Despite that, he looked relaxed, as if a prospective stint in the cooler was little more than a camp vacation.

McCain licked his lips and entered the interview room. "Hey, Pappy."

Delveccio glared at him. "I ain't talking to you."

"Why not? Am I that ugly?"

"Yeah, you are that ugly. But I also ain't talking to you 'cause I don't talk to cops."

"Sooner or later, you're gonna have to talk to us. I just

thought if it was just like you and me—you know, a little game of one-on-one—it makes things simpler."

Delveccio laughed. "Go fuck yourself."

McCain wagged a finger. "Yeah, you think about that when the needle slips into your veins."

Delveccio sneered. "No death penalty in Massachusetts. And all they're gonna charge me with is mischief or some shit like that."

"Who told you that?"

"Everybody."

"Well," said McCain, settling in a chair and winking, "you're right about the needle, but maybe you're gonna be wishing for the needle after fifty years in prison. Know what I'm saying?"

Delveccio laughed. "You're full of shit."

"And you are in trouble, my man. Because today's a new day and guess what, Pappy? We got the gun. Nice clear ballistics match to the bullets in Julius and a beautiful fingerprint match to you. It's first-degree murder now, Pappy. We're handing you to the DA, signed, sealed, and delivered."

Delveccio pursed his lips but didn't say anything. McCain decided to wait him out.

Finally: "Julius didn't die of no gunshot. You got nothing on me."

"That what they told you?" McCain shook his head. "Everyone's telling you stuff, and then stuff changes." His turn to laugh.

Delveccio tried to stay cool, but his youthful impulsiveness broke through. "What's so fucking funny?"

"Nothing," McCain said. "I don't blame you, Pappy. Most athletes do very well at trial. All those girls swooning over you." He paused. "But then again, most athletes don't have their fingerprints on the smoking gun. And most athletes don't kill other athletes. People liked Julius. Maybe more than you."

"It don't matter 'cause he didn't die from no bullet."

"You keep telling yourself that, Pappy. Maybe eventually, you'll convince someone." McCain stood. "Nice talking to you. Good luck with your lawyer."

He started for the door.

"Hey!" Pappy shouted.

McCain turned but didn't speak.

"You're lying," said Pappy.

McCain started to swivel back toward the door.

Pappy said, "What're you saying? What do you know about all this shit?"

"Sorry," McCain said. "I can't tell you anything without your lawyer present."

"Fuck my lawyer. What're you saying?"

McCain stuck a hand in his pocket. "Why should I tell you anything when you're not telling me anything?"

"'Cause . . ." Delveccio pursed his lips. "You're fixing me. I don't play fixed games. Yeah, I am gonna wait for my lawyer."

"Good choice," said McCain. "I hope for your sake he's not one of those guys trying to make his career outta you."

He headed for the exit. Had his hand on the doorknob when Delveccio said, "Maybe I can give you something. 'Cause I didn't do nothing. And that's the truth."

McCain kept his back to the boy.

"You hear me?" said Pappy.

McCain turned again, made eye contact. Saw Pappy's eyes flicker. The kid licked his lips, then his soul patch.

"What?"

"Sit down," said the kid. Ordering McCain like he was used to it. "I don't like you over me like that."

McCain sat.

"Here's the deal," said Delveccio. "I ain't saying nothing about what happened at the club. I ain't stupid." He leaned across the table. *Far* across. McCain's instinct was to recoil, but he held fast. Waited.

The kid said, "What I'm saying got nothing to do with Julius. It's got to do with something else."

"I'm listening." McCain tried to keep his voice even. It wasn't easy with that big scowling mug inches from his face.

Delveccio said, "Tell me what you'll give *me*."

"Can't do that until I know what we're talking about, Pappy."

"Man, you fixing me."

"Tell you what, Pappy. Give me a hint."

Delveccio sank back in his chair and folded his arms across his chest. "I might have an idea where a certain person that you been lookin' for is hiding."

"That so?" McCain's voice was even, but his brain was racing.

"Not that I know for sure," Delveccio said, "but I hear things."

"Speak to me."

"I don't do no time, okay?"

"That's not gonna happen, Pappy."

"Well . . . then I do the minimum. Six months for reckless firearm, whatever. City jail time, I can do that. I did that when I was fourteen."

"That so?"

"Yeah." Pappy grinned. "Got into a little fight with some dudes. Long time ago. Juvey record's all sealed."

"As it should be," said McCain.

"Three months," said Pappy. "I get back in time for the season."

"The boy died, Pappy. I got to be honest with you. But I'm not saying we can't work something out if you give me something good."

"Believe me, it's good."

"Look, Pappy, I'll do my best. What are we talking about?"

Delveccio grinned. "You're looking for someone, right?" He made kissy noises. "Mr. Lover Boy. And that's all I'm gonna say until you get me a deal."

McCain stared at him.

Looking for someone.

Lover Boy.

The bastard was talking about their multiple-murder fugitive wanted in Perciville, Tennessee.

The bastard was talking about Romeo Fritt.

14

By half past nine, both Pappy and Lover Boy were secured behind bars. Tomorrow, Romeo Fritt would be on his way back to Tennessee, where he could get the needle. And Delveccio would board a bus to jail.

Pappy's lawyers, upon hearing about the conversation with McCain, had tantrumed, threatened, then realized their boy had gotten a good deal. After three hours of wrangling with Harriet, the charge was involuntary manslaughter. Pappy's sealed youth record notwithstanding, he was a first offender. He might see playing time within a couple of seasons.

Dorothy and McCain weren't wild about the conclusion. But Change's assertion was still death by aneurysm, and it would have been impossible to get a premeditated-murder conviction.

Even attempted murder was a stretch.

"It's Boston," McCain said. "You gotta know your audience. I think we did fine."

Dorothy tightened her coat around her body. A bitter wind was whipping from the bay. The sky was dark and clear. No snow tonight, but that only made it colder. Her teeth chattered as she talked. "It isn't going to sit right with Ellen Van Beest."

McCain wrapped his scarf around his neck, mouth, and nose. "Pappy's still gonna serve time, and we got a worse murderer off the streets."

"I can't understand what you're saying."

He pulled the scarf off his mouth and repeated himself. "All in all, it's not too bad, right?"

"Yeah . . . How about you take Ellen's phone call?"

McCain was silent for a moment as he retrieved the car keys from his pocket. "Let's go out to dinner. I'm starved."

"I want to get home to the boys."

"Let's take them out," McCain said. "My treat. I'm thinking lobster. How about Legal?"

Dorothy couldn't resist that. "You know, I am hungry. I'll call up the boys and have them meet up with us."

"Sounds great." McCain opened the car door, shivering as he turned on the ignition and the heat. It took several minutes for the interior air to be breathable. "At first, I wasn't looking forward to Christmas in Florida. You know how I feel about Florida. Now after trudging through this cold spell and not sleeping for the last couple of days, Florida doesn't sound half bad."

"Take me with you."

"You're welcome to come."

Dorothy fished her phone from her oversize tote. She

looked at the cell's window and read her text message. "Forget lobster. Change wants to see us right away."

McCain groaned. "It's over."

"Apparently not. Want me to ignore the head ghoul?"

"Yeah," McCain said. "No." He snatched the phone from her. "Call him back but do it *after* dinner."

The basement lab was pitch-dark until Change flicked on the fluorescent lights. The ceiling fixtures blinked in succession until the room was awash in glare. After Dorothy's eyes adjusted, she took off her coat and hung it on the rack. Then she changed her mind and put it back on. It was an igloo inside.

Change said, "Evening, Detectives."

"Just don't tell me Julius died of a gunshot wound. Pappy's been dealt down."

"No, he didn't die of a gunshot wound." Change switched on the lights to a wall box mount, then searched through a series of large manila envelopes. "Sorry about the temperature. This shouldn't take long at all."

"So why couldn't it wait until the morning?" McCain grumped.

"I thought you might want to see this," Change said. "It could change your schedule for tomorrow."

McCain mumbled, "Then show it to us tomorrow."

Dorothy nudged him in the ribs. "What is it, Doc?"

"Here we go." Change pulled a large X-ray out of an envelope and placed it on the backlit monitor.

"A chest X-ray," McCain said.

"Exactly."

"You found the aneurysm?" said Dorothy.

"No aneurysm. But now more than ever, I believe that Julius died of one." Change picked up a pointer. "It should have been right around here. See this area of gray, this arch? This is where the aorta splits into the subclavian and the carotid."

"I don't see nothing except a bunch of ribs," McCain groused.

"We'll get to that in a moment," Change said. "There's nothing anatomically suspicious in this radiograph. Everything looks normal— No, let me modify that. Everything looks normal in the vascular department." He turned to McCain. "So since you're focused on the ribs, let's look at the ribs. Twelve ribs in all."

"Looks to me like a lot more than twelve," McCain said.

"That's 'cause you're seeing a double image. Ten ribs are attached. They come from the spine, swing around, and attach to the sternum." He picked up a pointer and traced. "Because the image is two-dimensional, what we're seeing is the same rib from both front and back projections."

"Got it," McCain said. "Go on."

"Here we have what we call the floating ribs—these projections on either side of the spine that appear to hang."

"And that's not normal?" Dorothy asked.

"No, that's very normal. Stay with me." Again, Change traced the ribs. "This twelfth rib is easy—nothing in its way. The eleventh rib in this X-ray is a little shorter than normal, meaning the tip is partially obscured by the rib cage, specifically by the tenth rib's arch. But if you look really carefully at what I'm pointing to, tell me what you see."

The detectives stared at the X-ray. McCain said, "It's like split."

"Yeah, yeah," Dorothy said. "I see it."

"It isn't *like* split," Change said. "It *is* split. It's called a supernumerary rib, in this case a bifid rib, and the condition is somewhat unusual but not really rare—one in twenty."

He faced them. "I autopsied the boy. I studied him from the inside out. The extra rib has nothing to do with Julius's death. But it also has nothing to do with Julius. This X-ray isn't from the body that I autopsied. The body I autopsied did not—I repeat did not—have a supernumerary rib. I would have seen it clearly, and I would have noted it."

Change's eyes heated. First time the detectives had seen that.

Dorothy said, "It's not Julius's X-ray."

Change said, "You're the detectives. You might want to find out what's going on."

Silence.

The ME tapped the X-ray with his pointer. "If I were you, I'd go back and look at all of Julius's medical records, not just those from his most recent year. "The one that the school gave seemed fine at the time, but now we'll want to see all of them. What was Julius, a senior?"

Dorothy nodded.

"So Boston Ferris Health Services should have other

chest radiographs. Go back and see if you can find different X-rays—at least one that really belongs to Julius."

He removed the film and placed it back in the manila envelope. "I'll keep this as part of my files."

"Oh my God, you know what this means, Dorothy?" McCain exclaimed. "It means we gotta go back to Boston Ferris and deal with Violet Smaltz."

Dorothy said, "This woman is impossible. She's just going to stonewall us—not because I think she has something to hide, but she loves drowning people in paperwork."

"I know the type," Change said. "Tell you what. I'll come with you. Maybe that'll speed things up."

"It would also speed things up if we enlisted President McCallum again," Dorothy said.

"He better help us out," McCain said. "Something's wrong at his damn school."

15

At eight in the morning, the campus was grayed by a heavy, moist sky. Somewhere behind the pewter mist the sun was trying to poke through, adding a little light but no warmth. The pathways that wound through the college were still slick with ice. McCain's boots crunched. His nose was brittle from the cold. He and Dorothy and Change had to work to keep pace with President McCallum.

"I'm sure it's an oversight." McCallum tightened his coat. "A simple mix-up." His voice lacked conviction. "It happens, you know. Mistakes in hospitals."

"This was a fatal mistake." McCain's teeth were chattering. "No doctor in his right mind would have allowed Julius Van Beest to play with a major aneurysm."

McCallum frowned and flung open the double glass doors to the health center, allowing the three of them to step inside. The waiting room was already packed with red-nosed, wan students, coughing, sneezing, slumping, shivering. The nurses greeted McCallum with surprise and deference as he blew past them and marched into the records room, where Violet Smaltz was worshiping her paperwork.

She looked up from her desk, her eyes darting back and forth between her visitors' faces. Then she stood up and tried to suppress a sneer. "President McCallum."

"Get me all of Julius Van Beest's medical records."

The woman went slack-jawed. "Sir, that's not standard procedure. I need permission—"

"The boy is dead!" McCallum shouted. "Get me his records, and get them *now!*"

Violet bit her lip. "It'll take a few moments."

"Then don't waste any more time!" McCallum bit his thumbnail. Inhaled, exhaled. Softened his tone: "It's of extreme importance, Violet. The reputation of the college hinges on it."

Smaltz nodded solemnly and disappeared behind the stacks of medical folders.

McCallum rubbed his hands together. "And you're positive, Dr. Change, that the X-ray that you saw couldn't possibly be that of Julius Van Beest?"

"One hundred percent positive."

"Well, then, we'll just wait and . . ." McCallum's voice faded.

No one spoke until Violet came back with the files. "These are all of them." She handed them to McCallum, who passed them to Change.

The ME pulled out the chest X-rays. "Do you have a light box?"

"Of course," said Violet. "We're not working out of tents, you know." She led them to an empty examination room and turned on the light box switch. Change mounted the X-rays to the clips and stared at the images.

It was McCain who spoke first. "The rib is still split."

"Indeed," Change said. "None of these images are of Julius."

"How can you be so sure?" McCallum challenged. "Isn't it possible he had surgery to remove the extra rib?"

Change considered the question. "When's he due to be buried?"

"He was buried yesterday," Dorothy said.

"I'll write out an exhumation order."

"Doc," said Dorothy, "maybe before we start unearthing the dead, we should think this out. First step: You're sure he died of an aneurysm."

"I would stake my reputation that this boy had some kind of preexisting vessel abnormality. And I see no reason for him to ever undergo surgery to remove a supernumerary rib. In fact, I'm certain he didn't—there were no old scars indicating such. These X-rays are not of Julius Van Beest."

Violet said, "I don't know if they're Julius's X-rays or not. But I'll tell you one thing. None of them were taken on school premises."

Four sets of eyes locked into hers. She pointed to markings at the bottom of the films. "Says here Professional Urban Imaging. I never even heard of this lab. Probably some fly-by-night operation, if you ask me."

McCain turned to the president. "Do most of the athletes have their chest X-rays done on school premises?"

"Why are you asking *him!*" Violet grumped. "I know the answer to that."

McCain waited.

"The answer is yes. Usually, the physicals are done two

weeks before school starts. I come in here to personally supervise the record keeping. I once left it to some subordinate, and boy was it a mess."

"I'm sure it took you hours to clean up," McCain quipped.

Violet gave him the force of her angry eyes, but she held her tongue. "Not only was this X-ray taken off campus but it was done late. Look at the date—a month after the semester started. That is *not* procedure."

Dorothy turned to Change. "You're saying no doctor in his right mind would permit Julius to play with an aneurysm."

"Correct."

"What if the team doctor hid it from Julius?"

"He'd have to be a psychopath," Change said.

"That's absurd!" McCallum protested. "Our staff is first-rate, and I will not tolerate such accusa—"

"Accusations or not," said Dorothy, "we'd be derelict if we didn't talk to the team doctor."

"I'm sure," said McCain, "that he'd be as concerned about this as we are. Seeing as he's first-rate and all."

McCallum grimaced. Stared at the ceiling. Threw up his hands. "I don't know if he's even on the premises."

"The coach is in," Dorothy said. "The team had an eight o'clock meeting today to talk about Julius. No exceptions. I'm betting that includes the team's doctor."

"So what are we waiting for?" Violet said.

"What are *we* waiting for?" McCain asked.

"The boy got his X-rays done off campus and as a result probably died from it. He shouldn't have been allowed to do that. This whole thing has impugned *my* record keeping and *my* system. That will not be tolerated!" Violet grabbed her coat from the rack. "Come on, people. Let's get the lead out."

The boys were working through some nominal drills, probably to keep up the appearance of normality. But Dorothy could tell by her son's drooped posture that he wasn't focused, and the others probably weren't, either. They were taking their cue from Coach Albert Ryan, a former Celtics journeyman and a twenty-year veteran of college coaching. Ryan, six-five and pole-thin and bald, normally a taciturn man, appeared paralyzed by the tragedy. His expression was captain-going-down-with-the-ship. When the group confronted him, he shook his head and pointed to a tall, paunchy man in his late fifties, wearing a blue blazer, gray slacks, and blue polo shirt, standing on the sidelines.

Martin Green was an orthopedic surgeon specializing in sports medicine. Besides running a full-time private practice, he'd been associated with Boston Ferris for fifteen years. He spoke with authority, but Dorothy could barely hear over echoing footsteps and ball bounces.

"Guys, maybe we can talk where it's a little quieter?"

McCallum said, "Coach, let's call it a day."

Ryan nodded and blew the whistle, told the boys to pack it in. Slowly, they filed out of the gym. Marcus acknowledged Dorothy with the faintest of nods but stuck with his teammates.

McCallum tapped his foot. Empty, the room reverberated like a cathedral.

Dr. Green said, "Julius insisted on getting his X-ray off campus. He was terrified of the procedure and wanted his own physician to do it."

"Afraid of X-rays?" said McCain.

"Apparently, his grandfather died of cancer due to excess radiation exposure. He didn't trust the school's machinery. Too much leakage or some such nonsense."

"Total nonsense!" Violet agreed.

"What kind of radiation exposure did this grandfather experience?" McCallum asked.

"Apparently, he worked as an assistant in a university lab." Green shrugged. "I never got the full story, and the little Julius did tell me seemed strange. But the upshot was Julius was anxious, and he'd already made plans to have his own lab take the X-rays. I saw no reason to argue with him."

"That's not procedure!" Violet chimed in.

"No, it is not," Green said. "But I didn't see the harm in it. He'd been doing it this way since high school. I actually called up the coach there, and at least that part of the story was true. Like most superathletes, Julius was super-particular. He had his superstitions, his rituals and routines, and I figured this was just another on a long list. Besides, as long as his chest X-ray was clean, what did it matter where it was taken?"

Change said, "So you examined the film."

"Of course. He handed it to me personally and we went over it together." Green's eyes darkened. "Why? What's going on?"

"Do you know how Julius died?" Change asked.

"He was shot."

"He was shot, but he died of a burst vessel, probably of the subclavian artery. I'm sure the kid had a preexisting aneurysm."

"Whoa, whoa, whoa," Green blurted out. "I never ever saw any aneurysm."

"That's because you didn't see an X-ray of Julius," Dorothy said.

Green was completely perplexed. "What are you talking about?"

Dorothy looked at Change, who explained the situation.

Coach Ryan broke in: "What the hell are you saying? That the whack to Julius's chest by that frickin' Duran is what caused his death?" He'd gone white and his face was sweat-drenched.

"Albert, sit down," Dr. Green told him.

"No, I'm fine! I want to know what's going on. Are you saying playing ball killed him?"

Change said, "Not exactly."

"Then what the hell are you saying?"

"Albert," said McCallum.

Ryan drooped. "Sorry, sir. My nerves . . ."

McCallum patted his shoulder. "We're all shaken up." He turned to Change. "Can we have a comprehensive explanation, please?"

Change said, "Precisely what caused the artery to burst would be speculation. What is clear is that Julius should not have been playing any type of contact sport."

"I wouldn't have let him play," said Green, "if I'd seen a damned aneurysm on a damned X-ray."

"See what happens when you don't follow procedure!" Violet broke in.

Everyone glared at her. But in this case, she happened to be right. Even McCain had to admit that.

He said, "If the kid's been doing this since high school, substituting one X-ray for another, it means he knew about his condition. So somewhere along the line, there's got to be an X-ray that showed an aneurysm."

"We can only go on what was given to us, people," McCallum stated. The relief in his voice was profound. "And these X-rays are clear. As far as we knew, the boy was healthy."

"They are clear and they are not of Julius."

Green said, "God, this is awful!"

"Detective McCain is right," Dorothy said. "There has to be an X-ray somewhere. The question is, how far back do we have to go?"

McCain said, "I bet his pediatrician has an X-ray from when he was a little kid."

"Which means he would have notified Julius's mother about it," Change said.

Dorothy said, "No mother in her right mind would let her son do something that would endanger his life. I'm positive Ellen didn't know about it."

"Is it standard procedure for a child to get a chest X-ray?" McCain asked.

Green said, "It isn't part of a routine childhood checkup. You don't want to expose kids to X-rays without reason. But with severe croup that doesn't resolve, a bad bronchitis, suspected pneumonia—sure, he could've taken a chest X-ray."

"Time to talk to Julius's pediatrician."

"We'd need Ellen's permission," Dorothy said. "I don't want to give her this kind of news right now. It's just too tragic." She looked at the team doctor. "Dr. Green, you said you spoke with the coach at Julius's high school and they had X-rays?"

Green nodded.

"Let's start there, compare their X-rays to these. At least we'll find out if he used the same substitute."

McCain said, "Where'd he go to high school?"

Coach Ryan said, "St. Paul's."

"St. Paul's in Newton?" Dorothy asked.

"Yes," President McCallum said. "Like most of our students, he was local."

McCain said, "Onward to Newton. Always liked the burbs in winter."

16

St. Paul's graced seven acres of rolling, high-priced Newton hills. The institution was basic New England prep. Episcopal school, but a sign on the colonial-era chapel said "Services are voluntary. Everyone is a child of God."

The head coach was Jim Winfield, another ex-NBA benchwarmer, nearly seven feet tall with a shaved head, a goatee, and the sculpted face of a Maori warrior.

Black *is* beautiful, thought Dorothy. What would it be like to live with a man with that kind of presence?

Like Ryan, Winfield seemed numbed by Julius's death. He told the detectives he did indeed remember a call from Boston Ferris inquiring about Julius Van Beest's chest X-rays.

"I don't remember if it was Dr. Green or Al Ryan. I know both of them quite well because over the past years, we've done lots of cross-referencing. So to speak."

They were sitting in his office, a generous, oak-paneled

space lined with trophy-stuffed display cases. The school had gone first place in football, basketball, baseball, soccer, hockey, tennis, swimming, polo, fencing, and lacrosse. St. Paul's took its athletics very seriously.

"And what did you talk about to whoever it was?" Dorothy asked.

"I don't remember the exact conversation, ma'am," Winfield said. "It was over three years ago. They wanted to know if Julius always brought in his own chest X-rays and I told him that *all* of our kids playing sports brought in their own. We don't have X-ray facilities."

There was a knock at the door. A hulking teenage boy, attired in gray flannel slacks, a white shirt, blue blazer, and rep tie, came into the office, carrying several manila envelopes.

Nice threads, thought McCain. Better than he'd ever worn, *including* at his own father's funeral.

"Ah . . . here we go," Winfield said. "Thanks, Tom. How's the ankle doing?"

"Better and better each day, Coach."

"Good to hear."

Tom smiled and left.

Winfield shook his head. "The kid twisted his ankle before a big game and played through the injury. What started out as a sprain turned into a torn ligament."

"That's terrible," Dorothy said. "Where were the parents?"

"I don't think they knew. These kids drive themselves crazy. They're all after the same scholarships, and the competition is fierce. It's terrible, but it's a fact of life." He handed the envelopes to Change. "Here you go, Doctor."

The ME said, "I'm surprised the school kept Julius's medical records this long."

"We keep everything for ten years, then it goes onto microfilm." Winfield smiled. "St. Paul's has a strong sense of history. A lot of alumni get famous, or at least well known."

Change pulled the radiographic image from Julius's senior year and held it to the window. The light wasn't perfect, but it was enough to illuminate the same bifid rib.

The detectives sighed in frustration.

"Are they all the same?" Dorothy asked.

"Let's find out," Change said. He took out another film.

"What are you looking for?" Winfield asked.

Change pointed to the supernumerary rib. "This is what we're looking for."

Winfield squinted. "Oh . . . I see. The bone is split. Does that mean anything?"

"It means that this isn't an X-ray of Julius Van Beest," Change said.

"What?" Winfield asked. "I'm confused. What's going on?"

"We wish we knew." McCain turned to Dorothy. "You tell him."

Winfield listened, his eyes widening in shock as Dorothy related the events of the last few days. When she was done, Winfield slapped his hand against his cheek. "Lord, I had no idea."

"Apparently, nobody did," Dorothy said. "Why would anyone assume the boy was trying to hide something?"

The third image was identical to the other two. McCain blew out air. "Looks like we're going to have to trace his medical history even further back." He looked at Winfield. "Any idea whose X-ray this is?"

"Not a clue."

Dorothy said, "Who did Julius hang with in high school?"

"He was a superstar," Winfield told them. "He had his fan club." The coach paused. "To tell you the truth, I was very pleased but also a little shocked when he chose college over the NBA. He was being scouted left and right. Everyone knew he had the stuff to make it in the pros. I always wondered why he didn't make the jump. Now I realize he must have known that pro sports would be a serious risk to his health. And he must have realized that his little charade wouldn't work in the majors. But even college sports . . . What was that poor boy thinking?"

"The boy was seriously misguided," McCain said. He paused a moment, then stared at the three radiographs. "Coach, is this a three-year or a four-year high school?"

"Four years."

Dorothy caught on. "Where's the fourth X-ray?"

"Julius transferred to St. Paul's in the middle of his freshman year."

"From where?" said McCain.

"I believe he was homeschooled for two months," Winfield said. "Before that he attended Lancaster Prep over in Brookline."

"Why'd he transfer?"

"We gave him a full scholarship, so I assumed that was the reason. Then I found out he had had a full scholarship at Lancaster, too, so the answer is I don't know. I always wondered what the story was, but . . . he did well here, and everyone was jazzed having him on board. We'd done well in every sport but b-ball. With Julius playing, that changed for the better."

Winfield sat back in his chair and sighed. "Maybe Lancaster knew, but I didn't." He shook his head. "This one hurts."

Lancaster Prep was a feeder for the Ivies. Its approach was old-fashioned, and its donors were old money. Episcopal, too, but here there was no opting out. The student population was well into its seventh generation of legacies, the exception being the athletes that Lancaster recruited hyperactively. Winning the yearly homecoming football game against Xavier was high-priority.

Yet another coach, yet another retired third-string basketball pro. Richard Farnsworth, a six-three guard who'd gone to fat, had played six seasons with eight different teams. By his own account, he was a workaholic, and it was unusual not to find him either in his office or on the court.

Farnsworth's office was compact and functional and also filled with trophies. He sat at his desk, ran his hand through shocks of curly gray hair, said, "Don't waste your time going through medical records. The school doesn't have them. When Julius left the school, his paperwork left with him."

"There was a problem," said Change.

Farnsworth scowled. "I was threatened with a huge civil lawsuit and dismissal if I spoke about it to anyone. Medical confidentiality and all that."

"The boy is dead, and this is a murder investigation," Dorothy said.

"What are you talking about?" said Farnsworth. "Julius was shot."

Change gave him the facts. Farnsworth looked ready to vomit. "Oh man—no, no, don't tell me that!" He pounded the table. "God, this is just sickening!"

McCain said, "What do you know about it, sir?"

Farnsworth grabbed a wad of tissues from a Kleenex box and slapped at his own face. "Goddammit! As soon as I got the report, I called up the parents and told them there was no way that the school would permit him to play basketball."

"You spoke to Ellen Van Beest?" Dorothy asked.

"No, no," Farnsworth said, "I talked to the old man— Leon."

"Leo," Dorothy corrected.

"Yeah. Right. Leo knew his kid shouldn't play. Leo himself was in the game a few years before me." Farnsworth's eyes clouded, shot back somewhere into his past.

Dorothy said, "So you spoke to Leo."

"I told him we needed to talk. He said the mother was busy working, so he'd come in. I told him Julius needed to be looked at by a specialist. He said he'd take care of it right away. I had no reason to doubt him. After all, it was his son, right?"

Farnsworth muttered under his breath.

"Soon after, he pulled the kid out of school. Said he was going to homeschool him while his medical problems were being tended to, some kind of operation. I thought that made a lot of sense. Julius was no dummy, but we didn't accept him on the basis of his test scores. So maybe a homeschool situation would be the best solution if he was going to be laid up."

"And Leo took the X-rays with him," said Dorothy.

Farnsworth nodded. "So he could get a second opinion. That made sense, too, right?"

The Coach cursed under his breath. "About three, four months later, I saw Julius playing for St. Paul's at the intramural games. My first thought was he must've had one hell of a surgeon. I was brooding over the fact that he didn't come back to Lancaster. Then, after mulling it over, I still thought that it was weird for Julius to be playing any kind of contact sport so soon after a major operation. Not that it was any of my business, but I called him up."

"Who?"

"Julius," Farnsworth said. "I think secretly I entertained hopes he'd come back to Lancaster if I sweet-talked him. The kid was as cold as ice. He said his medical problem was taken care of. Thank you. Good-bye."

He licked his lips. "Something was off. I called the old man and he cussed me out left and right, said if I interfered in his son's business, he'd make trouble for me. He said if I told anyone about anything, I'd be breaching confidentiality and he'd own my kids and my house." He threw up his hands. "It wasn't like the boy didn't know."

Dorothy said, "You didn't think of calling up his mother?"

"I thought the boy was living with his old man. I thought that if I told the mother and the old man had custody, he'd make good on his promise and slap me with a lawsuit." Tears welled up in Farnsworth's eyes. "I didn't think about it too hard because Leo was Julius's father."

He pounded the table again. "I don't know *what* I was thinking."

"You were thinking that Leo had his son's best interest at heart," Dorothy said.

Farnsworth nodded, grateful for the out.

"You were thinking that no father would intentionally put his son in harm's way."

"Correct. That's it to a T."

"You were thinking that if Julius was playing, he must have been strong enough to play."

"Yes, yes, exactly!"

"You were thinking all the right things," Dorothy said. "Unfortunately, your conclusion was still wrong."

17

Two-thirty in the afternoon and already Leo Van Beest was deep into alcoholic memories.

Back to the days when he'd been a Ferrari. For a while, the ride had been fast, wild, dangerously thrilling.

Now two detectives were standing over him and the dream was gone and Leo was feeling mighty sorry for himself.

His house was a one-bedroom, shingle-front dump, unkempt and unloved with dirty ice for a front yard. A rusted green Mercedes diesel sedan sat in the sunken driveway.

Inside, threadbare carpeting covered the floor, and bedsheets draped the windows. There were crusted dishes in the sink, and rumpled clothing and wrinkled papers were scattered everywhere. A rotten smell permeated the stifling front room. The walls were yellowed, hung with black-and-white photos from Leo's European glory days. The old man was dressed in torn sweats, drinking from a coffee mug, staring into the cup. A boozy steam wafted up from the rim and misted his face.

"I wouldn't have done it, 'cept that's what Julius wanted."

Dorothy said, "Parents are supposed to talk children out of bad decisions, Mr. Van Beest."

Leo looked up from his drink. Red eyes struggled to focus on Dorothy's face. He was sitting, but Dorothy was standing. No way she was going to touch that couch. Who knew what he had done on it?

"You think it was a bad decision, huh?" The old man sipped his drink. "I supposed to talk my son out of being someone big . . . someone famous. So he can do back-breaking labor for the rest of his days?"

"There were other options," McCain said.

Leo smiled, then laughed. "Oh, yeah. Other options. Like college. Like Julius was some kind of smarty." He laughed again, but it was mirthless. "That boy was born to *move*—born to run and jump and be a star. He was a race-horse, not an old plow horse. Julius was a *giant*! He was big and strong and coordinated and had a talent that was given to God's creatures once in a lifetime. That boy was a giant even with the giants. And I supposed to tell him he can't do it?"

He shook his head no, then he looked up again.

"You wanna know what the boy said to me? He said, 'Pops, I'd rather be a shooting star than no star at all. You gotta keep this a secret. You gotta not tell Mama, no matter what! You gotta be a man about this, Pops. And you gotta let *me* be a man.'"

"That your definition of being a man?" McCain said. "Knowing every time your son went on the basketball court, he could drop dead?"

"And a cop don't look death in the eye every time he answers a call?"

"That's a cheap shot," Dorothy said.

"No, you don't understand!" Leo said forcefully. He jabbed his finger up in the air. "You're a cop, that's your job. Julius was a basketball player. That was *his* job! And I be damned if I wasn't gonna let him live out his dream."

"His dream or your dream?" Dorothy said.

"Don't matter now," Leo snarled at her. "Because now it's nobody's dream."

No one spoke.

"I know what you all is thinking: that I killed my son by lettin' him play. Bullshit! Better he die a quick death than a slow painful one, you know what I'm saying?"

"No, I don't know what you're saying, sir," Dorothy said. "But that's irrelevant. If Julius had died in high school, I would have arrested you—for endangering the life of your child, maybe even for murder. But Julius died three years after he reached his majority. He knew his situation and he knew it was dangerous. At some point, it was his responsibility."

Leo nodded in agreement. "You're right about that, lady. The boy wanted to play no matter what."

"That's why he brought in X-rays of your chest instead of his," McCain said.

Leo didn't answer.

"Those were your X-rays, weren't they?" Dorothy said.

"My boy asked me to help him and I did," Leo said.

Dorothy's hands tightened into fists. He just didn't *get* it.

McCain said, "You helped your son nail his own

coffin, Mr. Van Beest. But like Detective Breton said, in the end it was Julius's decision."

"So what happens now?" said Leo.

"Legally, you're off the hook," Dorothy said. "But morally . . ." She didn't finish the sentence. "We're going now. If you want to contact us about anything, I can be reached at this number." She handed him her card.

Leo pursed his lips and tossed it aside. "Why would I want to talk to you?"

"You never know," McCain said.

"Does Ellen know how the boy died?"

McCain nodded. "She knows he died of an aneurysm."

"But she don't know the full story?"

Dorothy said, "We see no reason to give her additional heartache. I'm not going to rat you out, if that's what you're worried about."

Leo digested that. Nodded and got up from the couch. "I'll walk you out."

"No need," McCain said. "The place ain't that big."

They closed the door and walked away silently, too depressed to talk. They were halfway down the driveway, just past the Mercedes, when they heard the gunshot.

It made the front pages of the *Globe* and the *Herald*. Leo had lived a bum life, but he died a heartbroken hero. Ellen Van Beest attended two funerals in one week, then she took an extended vacation to be with her family.

"I could use that," Dorothy told McCain. "An extended vacation. As a matter of fact, I'd go for any kind of vacation."

"It's only two p.m." He closed his suitcase. "You still

got time to take the boys and come down to Florida with me. We can celebrate together."

"Micky, Christmas is snow on the treetops, a big roaring fire, and spicy, hot rum. Not palm trees and a sunburn."

"You burn?"

"Only when stupid people get on my nerves."

McCain grinned. "There's rum in Miami, pard."

She rolled her eyes and checked her watch. Micky's plane was supposed to depart in an hour. Unlike most airports, Logan International was located close to the city center—the one good thing about the place. Still, the roads were icy and traffic was always a bitch, especially on Christmas Eve. "We'd better get going, Micky."

He hefted his suitcase. "Let's do it, Detective."

Though the road was snarled and the tempers were hot, Dorothy made decent time. She watched Micky disappear into the terminal, then hooked back onto the highway for the ride back. All she wanted to do was get home and hug her kids.

Three blocks from her house, it started to snow . . . a gentle dusting. Soft snow, the kind that tickles your nose and face, the kind that makes you want to stick out your tongue and eat it. The kind of snow that turns dirty old Boston into a picturesque, quaint New England town.

Dorothy blinked and felt her cheeks go wet.

It was going to be a beautiful Christmas. She had to believe that.

DOUBLE HOMICIDE
SANTA FE

DOUBLE HOMICIDE

SANTA FE

JONATHAN & FAYE KELLERMAN

WARNER BOOKS

NEW YORK   BOSTON

Copyright © 2004 by Jonathan Kellerman and Faye Kellerman

Warner Books

Time Warner Book Group
1271 Avenue of the Americas, New York, NY 10020

Printed in the United States of America

ISBN 0-7394-4758-0

Book design and text composition by L&G McRee

To our children
Jesse and Gabriella Kellerman
Jonathan and Rachel Kessler
Ilona Kellerman
Aliza Kellerman

Special thanks to Michael McGarrity,
Santa Fe, New Mexico, police chief Beverly Lennen, and
Detective Sgt. Jerry Trujillo.

Still Life

1

Darrel Two Moons and Steve Katz were having a late dinner at Café Karma when the call came in. The restaurant was Katz's choice. Again. Two Moons watched his partner put aside his Eden-Yield Organic Lamb Plus Eclectic Veggie Burrito with great reluctance and fiddle in his pocket for his chirping pager.

It was just after ten-thirty p.m. Probably another south side domestic violence. For five weeks running, Darrel and Katz had worked the four p.m. to two a.m. Special Investigations shift. Their calls had consisted of feuding spouses, gang assaults, various and sundry alcohol-related issues, all taking place below St. Michael's—the Mason-Dixon Line that split Santa Fe and was more than an arbitrary map squiggle.

It was three weeks before Christmas, and the first few days of December had signaled an easy winter, with daytime temperatures in the forties. But four days ago, the weather had taken a drop: fifteen degrees Fahrenheit at night. The snow that had fallen during this serious drought year remained white and fluffy. The air was cold and biting. Their shift was one big freezer burn.

At least the weirdos who ran Café Karma kept the dive warm. Downright hot. A big and tall kind of guy to begin with, Darrel was drowning in clothing, sweating in his black wool shirt and black tie, black corduroy sports coat, and heavy black gabardine slacks tailored in Germany and inherited from his father. His quilted black ski jacket was draped over a horribly hand-painted chair, but he kept the sports coat on to conceal the department-issue .45 in its X-harnessed cowhide shoulder holster. No problem hiding his unauthorized boot gun, a nickel-plated .22. It nuzzled his calf, snug in his left custom-stitched elephant-hide Tony Lama.

Katz had on what he'd worn every night since the weather had turned: a fuzzy brown and white plaid Pendleton shirt over a white cotton turtleneck, faded blue jeans, black and white high-top sneakers. Over his chair was that ratty gray wool overcoat—pure New *Yawk.* How could he keep his feet warm in those Keds?

Two Moons sipped coffee and ate his dinner as Katz finally freed the now-silent pager. Over by the pastry case, the multipierced Goth waitress who'd served them—or tried to—stood gazing into space. She'd taken their order with vacant eyes, then had proceeded to the coffee machines, where the detectives watched her spend six straight minutes foaming Katz's Green Tea Chai Latte. Six and a half, to be precise: The detectives had timed her.

Staring into the foam, like it held some kind of big cosmic secret.

Darrel and Katz had exchanged knowing glances, then Two Moons had muttered under his breath about

4

what was really cooking in the back room. Katz had cracked up, his big red mustache rising and falling. This month, another team was handling narcotics.

Katz studied the number on the pager and said, "Dispatch." A bit more fumbling in another pocket and he produced his little blue cell phone.

Another meal cut short. Two Moons ate fast as Katz called in. He'd ordered as close to normal as possible at this loony bin: a mushroom burger with chipotle-spiced home fries and sliced tomatoes. Specifying no sprouts, but they'd stuck a tumbleweed of the stuff on his plate anyway. Darrel hated it; it reminded him of cattle fodder. Or something picked out of a comb. Just looking at it made him want to spit. He removed it and wrapped it in a napkin, whereupon Katz immediately grabbed it and snarfed it down.

If it were up to Katz, they'd be here every night. Darrel conceded that the food was consistently good, but atmosphere was another issue. With its snaky walkway embedded with pebbles and shards of mirror glass, antiwar petitions tacked to the Technicolor walls of the tiny entry, and cell-like rooms full of mismatched thrift shop furniture and incense fumes, Karma was what his gunnery sergeant father used to call "hippie-dippie left-wing lunacy crap."

Somewhere along the way, his father had changed, but Darrel's army-brat upbringing stuck with him. Give him a burger and plain old fries in politically neutral surroundings.

Katz reached dispatch. The office had been moved out of Santa Fe PD to the county building on Highway 14—police, fire, city, county, everything integrated—and most of the dispatchers were no longer familiar voices. But this time was different: Katz smiled and said, "Hey, Loretta, what's up?"

Then his face grew serious, and the big copper-wire mustache drooped. "Oh . . . Yeah, sure . . . Where? . . . You're kidding."

He hung up. "Guess what, Big D?"

Darrel chomped on his burger, swallowed. "Serial killer."

"Half correct," said Katz. "Just a killer. Blunt-force homicide on Canyon."

Canyon Road was very high-rent, just east of the Plaza in the Historic District, a narrow, leafy, quiet, *pretty* place lined with gated compounds and galleries and expensive cafés. The hub of Santa Fe's art scene.

Darrel's pulse rate quickened from forty to fifty. "Private residence, right? Not a gallery at this hour."

"Oh, a gallery, amigo," said Katz, standing and sliding into the ratty gray coat. "Very much a gallery. The d.b.'s Larry Olafson."

2

Hands encased in buckskin gloves, Two Moons drove, gripping the wheel as the car coasted down Paseo de Peralta, the main street that horseshoed around the city center. Snowdrifts lay across the piñon branches and juniper brush, but the road was clear. It was three weeks before Christmas, and the *farolitos* with their muted sepia candlelight rested on rooftops all over the town. As usual, the trees in the Plaza had been strung with multicolored lights. Still plenty of time, Darrel figured, to head over to the outlets and buy presents for Kristin and the girls—if he could ever get some time off.

And now this.

Of all people.

Lawrence Leonard Olafson had hit Santa Fe ten years ago like one of those sudden summer storms that shatter the sky in midafternoon and turn the desert air electric.

Unlike a summer downpour, Olafson had stuck around.

The son of a teacher and a bookkeeper, he'd attended Princeton on scholarship, graduated with a BA in finance and a minor in art history, and surprised everyone by eschewing Wall Street. Instead, he'd taken an entry-level scut job at Sotheby's—gofering for a haughty American Paintings specialist. Learning what sold and what didn't, learning that art collecting could be a disease for some, a pathetic attempt to social-climb for others. Kissing butt and fetching coffee and making the right kind of friends and moving up quickly. Three years later, he was department head. A year after that, he negotiated a better deal at Christie's and took a bevy of rich clients with him. Another eighteen months and he was managing a white-glove gallery on upper Madison, selling European as well as American. Cementing more connections.

By age thirty, he owned his own place in the Fuller Building on West 57th, a high-ceilinged, softly lit vault where he peddled Sargents and Hassams and Friesekes and Heades and third-rate Flemish florals to Old Money and Slightly Newer Money Pretending to Be Old Money.

Within three years, he'd opened his second venture: Olafson South, on 21st Street in Chelsea, heralded by a soiree covered in the *Voice*. Lou Reed music, sunken-eyed Euro-trash, prep school arrivistes, and neo-moneyed dot-commers vying for cutting-edge contemporary *pictures*.

Juggling both locations, Olafson made a fortune, married a corporate attorney, had a couple of kids, and bought a ten-room, park-view co-op on Fifth and 79th. Solidified yet more connections.

Despite a few rough patches.

Like the trio of Albert Bierstadt Yosemite paintings sold to a Munich banking heir that was most likely the work of a lesser painter—the experts' best guess was

Hermann Herzog. Or the unsigned Richard Miller garden scene unearthed at an Indianapolis estate sale and flipped overnight to a Chicago pharmaceuticals heir who displayed it in his Michigan Avenue penthouse with great hubris until the painting's provenance was shown to reek.

There'd been a few more misadventures over the years, but each incident was tucked safely away from the media because the purchasers didn't want to look stupid. Besides, Olafson had been quick to take the paintings back and make full restitution, offering sincere apologies and claiming honest error.

Everything was going swimmingly until middle age took root, a time when everyone who was anyone in New York went through some kind of life-enhancing, soul-altering major spiritual change. At forty-eight, Olafson found himself divorced, estranged from his children, restless, and ready to conquer new vistas. Something quieter, and though he'd never abandon New York, Olafson had begun to crave a clear contrast to the New York *pace*. The Hamptons didn't cut it.

Like any serious art person, he'd spent time in Santa Fe, browsing and buying and dining at Geronimo. Picking up a few minor O'Keeffes and a Henning that he turned over within days. Enjoying the food and the ambience and the sunlight, but bemoaning the lack of a seriously good hotel.

It would be nice to have his own spread. Bargain real estate prices clinched the deal: For one-third of what he'd paid for his co-op ten years ago, he could get an estate.

He bought himself a six-thousand-square-foot heap of adobe on five acres in Los Caminitos, north of Tesuque, with low-maintenance landscape and a rooftop-deck view of Colorado. Decorating all thirteen rooms with finesse, he set about filling the diamond plaster walls with art: a few Taos masters and two O'Keeffe drawings brought from Connecticut to get the tongues wagging. Mostly, he went in a new direction: neophyte contemporary Southwest painters and sculptors who'd sell their souls for representation.

Strategic donations to the right charities combined with lavish parties at the mansion cemented his social position. Within a year, he was *in*.

His physical presence didn't hurt, either. Olafson had known since high school that his size and his stentorian voice were God-given resources to be exploited. Six-three, lean, and broad-shouldered, he'd always been thought of as handsome. Even recently, with his hair gone but for a white fringe and a ponytail, he cut a fine figure. A cropped, snowy beard gave him the look of confidence. Opening night at the opera, he circulated among the rich in his black silk suit, collarless white silk shirt fastened at the neck by a turquoise stud, custom ostrich-leg clogs worn without socks, a young brunette on his arm, though the whispering class asserted this was pretense. For serious company, it was rumored, the art dealer preferred the lithe young men he hired as "groundskeepers."

Santa Fe had always been a liberal town in a conservative state, and Olafson fit right in. He threw money at an assortment of causes, some popular, others less so. Recently, less so had dominated: Olafson had made the papers after joining the board of an environmental group named ForestHaven and spearheading a series of lawsuits against small ranchers grazing on federal land.

That particular cause had generated lots of acrimony; the papers ran a couple of mom-and-pop-struggling-to-make-ends-meet heart-tugging articles. When asked to comment, Olafson had come across arrogant and unsympathetic.

Steve Katz brought up the story as he and Two Moons drove to the scene.

"Yeah, I remember," said Darrel. "I'd be pissed, too."

Katz laughed. "No sympathy for the sanctity of the land, chief?"

Darrel motioned at the windshield. "The land looks just fine to me, rabbi. My sympathy is with regular folk working for a living."

"You don't think Olafson worked for a living?" said Katz.

"Doesn't matter what I think or what you think," Two Moons snorted. "Our job is to figure out who bashed his head in."

Olafson Southwest sat atop a sloping lot on the upper end of Canyon, well past the gourmet aroma streaming from Geronimo and the U-pay outdoor parking lot run by the city to capitalize on tourists' SUVs. The property was large and tree-shaded, with gravel paths and a fountain and a hand-fashioned copper gate. In back was an adobe guesthouse, but the building was dark and locked, and no one was able to tell Katz and Two Moons if anyone actually lived there.

The gallery was divided into four whitewashed wings and a large rear room filled with paintings and drawings in vertical racks—what looked to be hundreds of pieces of art. The detectives drifted back. All that pale plaster and the bleached floors and the halogen lights positioned between the hand-hewn vigas lining the ceiling created a weird pseudo-daylight. Katz felt his pupils constrict so hard his eyes hurt. No sense browsing. The main attraction was in room number two. The body was laid out where it had fallen, stretched across the bleached pine floor.

A big, nasty still life.

Larry Olafson lay on his stomach, right arm curled beneath him, the left splayed and open-fingered. Two rings on the hand, a diamond and a sapphire, and a gorgeous gold Breguet watch on the wrist. Olafson wore an oatmeal-colored woolen shirt, a calfskin vest the color of peanut butter, and black flannel slacks. Blood splotched all three garments and had trickled onto the floor. Buckskin demi-boots covered the feet.

A few feet away was a piece of sculpture: a huge chrome screw on a black wooden base. Katz inspected the label: *Perseverance.* An artist named Miles D'Angelo. Two other works by the same guy: a massive screwdriver and a bolt the size of a truck tire. Behind those, an empty pedestal: *Force.*

Katz's ex-wife had figured herself for a sculptor, but it had been a while since he'd talked to Valerie or any of her new friends, and he'd never heard of D'Angelo.

He and Darrel got close to the body, and they both inspected what had once been the back of Larry Olafson's head.

Tan, hairless skin had been turned to mush. Blood and brain tissue crusted the white fringe and the ponytail. Stiffening the hair, turning it deep red, a blood henna job. A few specks of blood, a light spray, had made it to a nearby wall, to Olafson's right. Serious impact. The air was coppery.

All of Olafson's untouched jewelry said robbery was doubtful.

Then Katz berated himself for limited thinking. Olafson trucked in high-end art. There were all kinds of robbery.

That empty pedestal . . .

The coroner, Dr. Ruiz, had stuck a thermometer in the liver. He looked at the detectives, then sheathed his instrument and inspected the wound. "Two, three hours tops."

Two Moons turned to the uniform who'd greeted them at the scene. She was a rookie named Debbie Santana, a former Los Alamos clerk on the job less than a year. This was her first d.b. and she looked okay. Maybe working with nuclear stuff was scarier. Darrel asked her who had called it in.

"Olafson's houseboy," Debbie replied. "He came by half an hour ago to pick up the boss. Apparently, Olafson was working late, meeting a client. He and the houseboy—Sammy Reed—were supposed to have dinner at ten, over at Osteria."

"Client have a name?"

Debbie shook her head. "Reed says he doesn't know. He's pretty hysterical, can't stop crying. He says he found the door locked, used his key, called out Olafson's name. When no one answered, he walked in and found it. No signs of forced entry. I guess that fits his story."

"Where's Reed now?"

"In the cruiser. Randolph Loring's watching him."

Katz said, "So it went down between eight and ten."

"Approximately," said Dr. Ruiz. "Stretch it on the front end to seven-thirty."

Two Moons left the room and returned a moment later. "The door says the gallery's open till six. Olafson must've thought the client was serious to stay two hours late."

"Or he got conned," said Katz.

"Either way, if he thought there was serious money involved, he'd stay as late as it took." Darrel bit hard on his lower lip. "That guy *loved* his money."

The hostility in the remark was out of place. Santana and Ruiz stared at Two Moons. He ignored the scrutiny and began checking out the paintings on the wall. A series of blue-gray abstractions. "What do you think of these, Steve?"

"They're okay," said Katz. He was still kneeling by the body. A little surprised by the hostility but not shocked. For the last few days, Darrel had been grumpy. It would pass. It always did.

He asked Dr. Ruiz about the bloodstains.

Ruiz said, "I'm no spatter expert, but there's no blood in any of the other rooms, so it's pretty obvious he got hit right here. Cracked right across the occiput—back of his head—over to the right. Looks like one blow. I don't see any signs of struggle. He got whacked and he crumpled."

"He's a tall guy," said Katz. "Was it an upward or a downward blow?"

"More like straight across."

"So we're talking about another big man."

"That seems logical," said Ruiz, "but I can tell you more after I cut him open."

"Any guesses about the weapon?" said Katz.

Ruiz thought a moment. "What I can say at this point is it was something big and heavy with rounded edges." He got down next to Katz and pointed at the pulpy wound site. "Look over here. One furrow but it went extremely deep. The impact shattered bone. There are no small fragments on visual, like you'd get with a sharp-edged instrument. No cut marks, period. Whatever was used inflicted damage over a comparatively wide surface and pushed the fragments down into the brain. Serious heft."

"Like a crowbar?"

"Larger. We're talking tremendous force."

"Lots of anger," said Darrel.

Ruiz got up and stretched. Touched his knee and winced.

"Sore, Doc?"

"Middle age sucks."

Katz smiled and cocked his head at the empty pedestal.

"I saw that," said Ruiz. "Could be. If it's like the others weightwise."

Darrel said, "Carrying away something that heavy would be tough. And there's no blood trail."

"If it's chrome," said Ruiz, "the blood might not have adhered in any degree—might've dripped off soon after impact. Or your murderer wiped it and took it with him."

"Souvenir?" said Darrel.

Ruiz smiled. "Maybe he's an art lover."

Katz smiled back. "Or he was hyped up, adrenalized, took it with him, and dropped it somewhere nearby."

Darrel checked his watch. "Time to search."

Katz said, "It's pretty dark out there, and I didn't see any outdoor lights near the guesthouse."

"No problem," Two Moons countered. "Let's cordon the entire property, get some night spots, block off upper Canyon."

15

Ruiz grinned. "You block off upper Canyon, you'd best finish early."

Wiseass smile, Katz noticed, which could be Ruiz's way when dealing with a body. A small, round, highly intelligent man, the Hispaniola-born son of a plasterer, David Ruiz had gone to UNM on scholarship, earned an MD from Johns Hopkins, served a forensic-path residency at New York Hospital. He'd spent a couple of years with Dr. Michael Baden in the New York ME's office. He and Katz had traded lots of New York war stories. The Santa Fe job had brought Ruiz back to his home state. He lived outside the city limits, on a ranchero near Galisteo, with horses and cows, dogs and cats, a couple of llamas. He had a wife who liked animals and a whole bunch of kids.

"Nine by the latest," Ruiz continued. "That's when the tourists start coming. Blocking off Canyon will turn you into civic impediments."

Two Moons spoke in his laconic voice. "And here I was thinking I was a civil servant."

"Consider this," said Ruiz. "A few hours ago, Olafson was an important man. Now *he's* an impediment."

The detectives had the techs dust for prints all over the gallery and in Olafson's rear office. Tons of latents showed up immediately, which was almost as bad as a blank screen. When everything had been photographed, they gloved up and checked out the art dealer's desk. In a top drawer, Katz found Olafson's Palm Pilot. Lots of names, a few he recognized. Including Valerie's. That surprised him. As far as he knew, she'd given up her art dreams, had reached a medium level of contentment working at the Sarah Levy Gallery over in the Plaza, selling high-end Pueblo pottery.

"These are people with real talent, Steve," she'd told him when he'd dropped by. "At least I'm smart enough to know the difference."

Katz had thought he spied moisture in the corners of her eyes. But maybe he was wrong. When it came to Valerie, he'd been wrong a lot.

Checking his gloves for pinholes and wrinkles, he scrolled through more names on the Pilot.

Two Moons said, "Too much stuff. This is going to be one of those. Let's tag and bag and we'll go through it later. Meanwhile, how about the houseboy?"

Sammy Reed was twenty-four, delicate, black, and still weeping.

"I can't believe it, I just can't believe it."

He asked to get out and stretch, and the detectives said sure. Reed wore a too big herringbone tweed overcoat with a black velvet collar that looked vintage. Black jeans, black Doc Martens, diamond chip in his right earlobe. As he flexed his arms and legs, they checked out his size.

Five-six in his Docs, maybe one twenty.

In the car once more, Two Moons and Katz flanked him in the backseat. The heater hummed intermittently, and the temperature hovered between chilly and passable. Reed sniffled and denied knowing whom "Larry" was staying late to meet. Olafson didn't discuss business details with him. His houseboy duties consisted of keeping the mansion neat and clean, doing some light cooking, taking care of the pond and the pool and Larry's borzoi.

"She's going to be heartbroken," he said. "Shattered." As if to illustrate, Reed cried some more.

Darrel handed him a tissue. "The dog."

"Anastasia. She's six. Borzois don't live that long. Now that Larry's gone . . . I can't believe I just said that. *Gone.* Ohmigod."

"Can you think of anyone who'd do this?"

"No," said Reed. "Absolutely not. Larry was beloved."

"Popular, huh?"

"More than popular. Beloved."

"Still," said Katz, "sometimes you run into difficult people."

"If Larry did, I don't know about it."

"He didn't talk business with you?"

"No," said Reed. "That wasn't my role."

"Who works at the gallery?"

"Just Larry and one assistant. Larry was trying to streamline."

"Financial problems?"

"No, of course not." Reed gulped. "At least none that I knew of, and Larry didn't seem to be worried or anything like that. Just the opposite. He was talking about buying more land. So he must've been doing okay."

"Land where?"

Reed shook his head.

Darrel said, "What's the assistant's name?"

"Summer Riley."

Katz remembered the name from the Palm Pilot. "Where does she live?"

"In the guesthouse out back."

The detectives said nothing, both of them wondering what lay behind the guesthouse door.

Darrel said, "Did Larry receive any threats you're aware of?"

Reed shook his head.

"Hang-up calls, weird mail, anything like that?"

Three more headshakes.

"Nothing out of the ordinary?" said Katz. "Especially within the last few weeks?"

"Nothing," Reed insisted. "Larry's life was tranquil."

"Tranquil," said Two Moons.

"I'm talking compared to his New York days," said Reed. "He adored Santa Fe. Once he told me his original plan had been to spend just a few months here, but he came to love it so much that he decided to make it his primary residence. He was even talking about closing up one of the New York galleries."

"Which one?" said Katz.

"Pardon?"

"He had two, right?"

"Yes," said Reed. "The one in Chelsea."

"West 21st—contemporary art," said Katz.

Reed's eyes were wide with surprise. "You've been there?"

"I used to live in New York. So Mr. Olafson was thinking of downsizing."

"I don't know for sure, but he mentioned it."

"When?"

"Hmm . . . a month ago maybe."

"What was the context?" said Katz.

"The context?"

"He didn't usually talk business with you."

"Oh," said Reed. "Well, this wasn't business. It was more . . . Larry was in a good mood, kind of . . . talkative . . . reflective about life. We were out on the *portal*—nighttime. Back when we had that warm spell?"

"Yeah, a month ago," Two Moons said. *More like a century ago in winter hours.*

"Where was I?" Reed asked.

"The *portal*," Katz clued him in.

"Yes, right," said Reed. "The *portal*. Larry was waiting for his dinner. Drinking wine. I'd cooked halibut in an olive sauce and penne with pistachios. After I brought the food to the table, Larry asked me to sit down and share with him. It had been a long day. Anastasia had some stomach problems. Larry said I deserved a break. So I sat and he poured me some wine and we chatted." Reed sighed. "It was a really clear night, all those stars. Larry said he felt spiritual in a way he'd never experienced back East." The young man's lip quivered. "Now *this*. I can't believe—"

"Closing up a gallery," said Katz. "What would that have meant for the artists he represented?"

Reed tried to shrug. Being the filling in a detective sandwich checked his movement. "I guess they'd find new representation."

"Except for the ones who couldn't," said Katz. "It's like that in the art world, right? C students versus A students. Some would have found themselves with no representation."

Reed stared at him. "I guess."

"You an artist?"

"No, no way, can't draw a straight line. I'm a cook. I trained to be a chef at the CIA—the Culinary Institute, up in the Hudson Valley—but mostly, I ended up being a cook. Actually, I ended up doing kitchen grunt work for minimum wage at Le Bernardin and places like that. So when Larry offered me a job in Santa Fe, I *leaped* at the opportunity."

"How'd Mr. Olafson find you?"

"I was daylighting for a very high-end caterer, but I

could tell you stories . . . Anyway, Larry threw a Sunday brunch at the gallery. I suppose I passed muster with the guests. The smoked pineapple and habanero-spiced prawns didn't hurt, either." Small smile. "He said he liked the way I handled myself."

"How long have you worked for him?"

"Three months."

"Enjoy it?"

"It's been heaven." Reed broke down and caught his breath long enough to plead for another tissue.

Another half hour of questioning proved unproductive. Reed denied a personal relationship with his boss, but he wasn't convincing. Katz caught Two Moons's knowing glance over the top of the houseboy's head.

Run him through the system before we let him go.

But neither of them felt it would amount to much. When the houseboy's preliminary arrest search came back clean, except for a speeding ticket two months ago on Highway 25 just outside of Albuquerque, no one was surprised. Reed was boy-sized, and the only way he could've smacked Olafson level across the head was if he'd stood on a ladder.

Not to mention wielding a heavy rounded instrument.

It was time to join the search for *that*.

Probably another dead end.

Katz and Two Moons stuck around for another hour and a half, supervising the boundaries of the cordon and the setting up of the night spots, working with three additional uniforms and two techs in the search of the property. A good chunk of Santa Fe PD's force was here. It was the first homicide for all the uniforms, and no one wanted to screw up.

They forced open the lock on the guesthouse door. No body inside, just a messy one-room studio. Summer Riley's personal effects, some weed and a bong in a night-stand drawer, an easel and a paint box in the kitchen, a bunch of really bad oils—crooked, ugly women rendered muddily—propped against the walls. On her bed was a pile of dirty clothes.

Two Moons found Summer Riley's cell phone number in Olafson's Palm Pilot, called her up, and got her voice mail. Sensitive guy that he was, he left a message for her to come home because the boss was dead.

It was Katz who found the murder weapon, lying under a creeping juniper, just off the pathway that led to the guesthouse.

No attempt to conceal. The thing had rolled to a low spot in the garden.

Big chrome ball-peen hammer, the size of a motor-cycle engine, streaked lightly with pink stains—the faint adherence that Dr. Ruiz had predicted. Couple of brain fragments on the peen. Precisely the wide, round surface that Ruiz had described.

Three techs struggled to bag and tag the hammer. Huge and cumbersome, it had to weigh sixty, seventy pounds. Meaning a *very* strong bad guy, even factoring in the adrenaline rush.

"Killed by art," said Darrel. "Wasn't there some guy, some painter, who once said his goal was to create a painting where you'd look at it and drop dead?"

"Never heard of that," said Katz.

"I learned it in class. The guy had a weird name—Man something."

"Man Ray?"

"That's the one."

"You took art?" said Katz.

"Art history," said Darrel. "In college. Because it was easy."

"Learn anything?"

"That I liked seriously pretty stuff as much as anyone, but seriously studying it was ridiculous."

"It's like everything else," said Katz. "God gives us good stuff and we make it complicated."

Darrel glanced at him "You're religious now?"

"I was talking . . . metaphorically."

"Ah," said Two Moons. "Well, the big metaphor tonight is 'dead as a doornail.' Any ideas?"

"Check out his house," said Katz. "Get hold of his phone records, find Summer Riley and see what she knows, talk to the ex-wife in New York, or wherever she is, learn more about Olafson's business. That ForestHaven deal, too. Be interesting to see what the ranchers he sued have to say."

"Sounds like a comprehensive plan, Steve."

They headed for the car.

Darrel said, "Way I see it, we'll be looking for enemies in all the right places. Something tells me we're going to be real busy."

Just as they were about to drive off, one of the uniforms said, "Look who's here."

Headlights flashed, then dimmed as a squad car drove up. Chief Shirley Bacon got out wearing a navy-blue knit pantsuit under a long black shearling coat, her dark hair piled and sprayed high, more makeup on her face than she ever wore at the station.

She was compact and open-faced, a forty-eight-year-old former teacher, daughter of a county sheriff and the sister of a state cop, another sheriff, and a probation officer. She'd started out playing the violin, ended up giving music lessons and working as a secretary at the opera while hoping for better. A broken hand at age thirty-five had sent her to the department as a secretary. One thing led to another and she joined SFPD.

She'd climbed fast by being smart and able, had made it to chief last year. She treated her officers with respect, got a sixty-mile vehicle take-home policy passed on their squad cars, and pushed through a salary raise in an era of budget-cutting. No one begrudged her a damn thing, no one thought about her gender.

She headed straight for them.

"Darrel, Steve."

"Big night out, boss?" said Katz.

"Fund-raiser. The Indian Art Foundation, Dr. and Mrs. Haskell's place, up on Circle Drive. What's the story here?"

They told her as she grimaced. She said, "This could go in all sorts of directions. I'll deal with the papers. Keep me posted."

Within moments, the chief's deputy, Lon Maguire, showed up in his off-duty truck, and soon after that, Lieutenant Almodovar joined the huddle.

No ideas from the bosses. But no anxiety or criticism, either. During Katz's three years with the department, he'd been impressed by the lack of backbiting and barely suppressed anger. All that good stuff he'd dealt with in New York. Then again, NYPD dealt with more homicides weekly than he'd seen in three years here.

Chief Bacon gave them a simple wave, then turned to leave.

"Back to the party, boss?" asked Katz.

"Heck no, that was about as boring as it gets." She shouted as she walked away, "But next time give me a simpler way to excuse myself!"

At 2:53, nearly an hour past shift's end, just as they were about to leave for Olafson's house, they spotted a good-looking young couple standing outside the cordon, at the far end, talking to Officer Randolph Loring.

They headed over and Loring said, "This is Ms. Riley. She lives out in back."

Summer Riley was raven-haired and ivory-skinned with a curvy shape even her bulky ski jacket couldn't conceal. Her big blue eyes were as scared as a cornered rabbit's. Katz put her at late twenties.

The denim-clad guy with her was tall, dark, handsome in that Latin-lover type of way. Brown wavy hair that fell past his shoulder blades and a pale, strong-boned face. Equally freaked-out.

Katz thought: This could be a Calvin Klein ad. Even the fear. *Especially* the fear.

Summer Riley hadn't picked up Two Moons's message. She was just returning from a date. Darrel gave her the same straight-out story he'd told her machine, and she collapsed into the young guy's arms. He held her, looking awkward. Stroked her hair with all the vitality of a robot.

His name was Kyle Morales, and he was a UNM dance major who worked part-time at the flamenco show over at the Radisson. He was on hiatus until spring of next year.

Katz had seen the show, sitting alone at the back of

the room with the single Tanqueray and tonic he allowed himself. Slightly apart from the rest of the audience, whose mean age had been about sixty-five.

He'd been pleasantly surprised by the show: good dancers, good guitar work. He said so to Kyle Morales.

Morales said, "Thanks," without any feeling.

When Katz said, "How about we talk to you guys separately?" Morales complied without fuss.

Darrel guided Summer Riley through the cordon, over to the guesthouse, while Katz stayed right there with Morales.

It was the second time Morales had gone out with Summer. He'd met her at a bar on San Francisco Street, thought she was "cool." He had no idea who Lawrence Olafson was and knew less than nothing about art.

"Second date," said Katz.

"The first was just drinks, kinda," said Morales.

"What about tonight?"

"Tonight we saw a comedy over at the DeVargas Center."

"Funny?" said Katz.

"Yeah," said Morales, not even trying to fake it. A dancer, not an actor.

"Then what?"

"Then we got a pizza. Then we were headed back here."

"First time at her place?"

"Supposed to be." Uttered with regret.

Tough luck, thought Katz. All chance of getting laid blown to bits by the nasty business of murder.

He questioned Morales awhile longer, deciding the guy wasn't very bright. Just another wrong place, wrong time situation.

26

"Okay, you're free to go."

Morales said, "I thought maybe once she was finished with you guys, we could still hang out."

"You can take your chances and wait," said Katz, thumbing the cordon tape, "but talking from experience, buddy, it's gonna get real cold."

In the end, Morales decided to pack it in. Katz joined Two Moons and Summer Riley in the single-room guest-house. Added to the previous disarray was a layer of print powder. The girl was drying her tears. It was hard to say if that was because of the situation or Darrel's sensitive approach—or both.

Darrel said, "Ms. Riley doesn't know anyone who'd want to harm Mr. Olafson."

"He was wonderful," sniffled Summer.

Darrel didn't respond and the girl said, "Like I said, you really need to check if any of the art's missing."

"Robbery," said Darrel, using his flat voice.

"It's possible," said Summer. "Larry *is* the top dealer in Santa Fe, and he's got some pretty expensive pictures in the gallery."

"O'Keeffe?"

"No, not at this time," said Summer defensively. "But we've sold several of them in the past."

"What's pricey now?"

"There's a gorgeous Henry Sharp Indian and some Berninghauses and a Thomas Hill. Maybe that doesn't mean anything to you, but they're valuable pictures."

"Sharp and Berninghaus were Taos masters," said Katz. "I didn't know Hill painted New Mexico."

Summer's head drew back as if his knowledge had assaulted her. "He didn't. It's a California scene."

"Ah."

"They're pricey. Six figures each."

"And he kept them in the gallery?" asked Katz.

"Except for what he takes home," said Summer, staying in the present tense.

"For his personal use?"

"He circulates art in his house. He inherently loves the art and also to have around for visitors."

"A sample," said Katz.

The young woman looked at him as if he'd uttered a vulgarity.

Darrel said, "Where in the gallery are these masterpieces stored?"

"With all the other pictures," said Summer. "In the storage room. It's got a special lock and alarm, and only Larry has the combination."

"Do you mean the back room?" asked Two Moons. "The one with all those vertical racks?"

Summer nodded.

The detectives had walked right in. The door had been left open. Katz realized he hadn't even noticed the lock. "Where would we find an inventory list?"

"On Larry's home computer," said Summer. "Also, I keep a written log for backup. I'm real good at organizing. That's why Larry likes me."

The state of her room said otherwise, but who knew.

Then Katz thought: She hadn't even bothered to clean up before bringing Kyle Morales back. Maybe her plans had been different from Morales's.

He asked her about the dancer. Her story matched Morales's.

Katz said, "So you and Kyle were headed back here."

Summer said, "He was taking me home." She tossed

her hair and blushed. "That was it. I wasn't going to see him again."

"Bad date?"

"Boring. He's not bright."

Metallic edge to her voice. This one could be tough.

"The artist who made the hammer—Miles D'Angelo," said Katz. "What can you tell us about him?"

"Miles? He's eighty-three and lives in Tuscany."

"Mr. Olafson have any conflict with him?"

"With Miles?" Summer smirked. "He's the gentlest man alive. He loved Larry."

Two Moons said, "We'll need a look at your log."

"Sure," said Summer. "It's back in the gallery. In Larry's desk."

The detectives hadn't seen anything like that.

They returned to Olafson Southwest, where the girl pointed to the drawer. Darrel gloved up and slid it open.

Papers but no log.

"It's not there," said Summer Riley. "It's supposed to be there."

3

By 3:10, Katz was at the wheel of the Crown Victoria with Two Moons silent in the passenger seat. They were headed north up Bishop's Lodge Road toward Tesuque, a flat and tree-shrouded village, an odd mix of horse estates and mobile homes, some nice-view houses of all sizes studding the hills that rimmed the town. The population was movie stars and financial types playing absentee rancher, artists and sculptors and horse people, the blue-collar Hispanics and Indians who'd been Tesuque's original residents. And then there were a few truly weird loners who skulked into the Tesuque Market to buy organic veggies and beer, only to disappear for weeks.

The kind of mix Katz would've thought volatile, but like the rest of Santa Fe, Tesuque stayed pretty calm.

The sky was jammed with stars—awash in diamond light—and the air smelled of juniper and piñon and horse manure. Lawrence Olafson's place was on a narrow dirt road well beyond the town limits, at the far, high end of the Los Caminitos tract, a posh neighbor-hood of big, pretty adobe dream houses on five-to-fifteen-acre lots.

No streetlights since they'd left the Plaza, and out here the darkness was a thick, tangible fudge. Even with high beams, the address was easy to miss: discreet copper numerals on a single stone post. Katz overshot, backed up, continued up the sloping drive, slick with patches of frozen water. Five hundred feet of dirt road swooped through a snow-topped piñon corridor. There was no sign of the house until the third turn, but when you saw it, you saw it.

Three stories of rounded angles, free-form walls, and what looked to be a half dozen open patios along with an equal number of covered *portales*. Pale and monumental against a mountain backdrop, lit subtly by the moon and the stars and low-wattage lighting, it was ringed by a sea of native grass and globules of cactus, dwarf spruce, and leafless aspen branches that shivered in the wind.

For all its size, the place was a harmonious fit with the environment, rising out of sand and rock and scrub like a natural formation.

Officer Debbie Santana's cruiser sat in front of the quadruple garage that formed the house's lowest level. It was parked perpendicular, blocking two and a half garage doors. Katz left the unmarked several yards away, and he and Two Moons got out and stepped onto crunchy gravel.

A climb up twenty stone steps took them past a river of shrubs to massive double doors hewn from wood that looked ancient. Nailhead borders, hardware of hand-hammered iron. Above the door a carved plank: HAVEN.

Darrel pushed at the door, and they stepped into an entry hall bigger than Katz's entire apartment. Flagstone floors, twenty-foot ceilings, some kind of free-form glass chandelier that he figured might be a Chihuly, peach-blush walls of diamond plaster, gorgeous art, gorgeous furniture.

Beyond the entry was a step-down great room with an even higher ceiling and walls that were mostly glass. Officer Santana sat on a tapestry sofa next to Sammy Reed. Reed had gone from weepy to numb.

Darrel said, "Nice place. Let's tear it apart."

They spent the next three hours going over six thousand square feet. Learning plenty about Olafson, but nothing that told them a thing about the murder.

A Jaguar sedan, green and sleek, resided in the garage, along with an old white Austin Healey and a red Alfa Romeo GTV. Olafson's Land Rover had been ID'd in the driveway of the gallery.

They pawed through closets full of expensive clothes, mostly with New York labels. Bankbooks and brokerage accounts said Olafson was more than solvent. Gay and straight porno was stacked neatly in a locked drawer of the media room. Plenty of bookshelves in the leather-walled study, but very few books—mostly coffee-table numbers on art and decorating, and biographies of royals. The borzoi, huge and fleecy white, slept through it all.

Art was everywhere, too much to take in during a single visit, but one painting in the great room caught Katz's eye: two naked children dancing around a may-pole. The pastel tints were of a mellow summer. The kids were around three and five, with fluffy yellow hair, dimpled buttocks, and cherub faces. Given the sappy theme, it could've been poster art, but the painter was skillful enough to elevate the image. Katz decided he liked it and checked the signature. Some guy named Michael Weems.

Two Moons said, "Think we should look for kiddie porn?"

That took Katz by surprise, shook him a bit. He checked his partner's face for irony.

"Eye of the beholder," said Two Moons, and he headed for Olafson's desktop computer.

The PC switched on, but the opening screen demanded a password and the detectives didn't even try.

Bobby Boatwright, a sex-crimes guy on the two to eight-thirty shift, was as good with machines as any techno-head. Let him have a go at it before they bundled it off to the state police forensic lab on Highway 14.

They unplugged the computer and took it along with the printer and battery pack into the entry hall. Then back to the private world of Lawrence Olafson.

Under the four-poster in the regal bedroom, they found a tooled-leather scrapbook. Inside were clipped articles about Olafson.

"What?" said Darrel. "He lulled himself to sleep with ego trips?"

They paged through the album. Most were puff pieces from art magazines, describing the dealer's latest auction, acquisition, or price-setting sale. But also there were negative pieces: whiffs of deals gone sour, questions about authenticity. Why Olafson kept those was anyone's guess.

Under the scrapbook was another volume, smaller, bound in cheap green grass cloth. That one held clippings about ForestHaven, including the *News-Press* story about the small-time ranchers sued by the group.

Bart Skaggs, sixty-eight, and his wife, Emma, sixty-four, had been targeted specifically because they struggled financially to raise five hundred head of beef cattle to market weight, using their federal grazing rights in Carson Forest as collateral against bank loans for feed and stock and equipment. Each year, the interest ate up $31,000 of their $78,000 gross income, but until ForestHaven brought the Skaggses to court using the Endangered Species Act, they'd managed to scrape by.

The suit claimed damage wrought by the Skaggses' herd was jeopardizing native rodents, reptiles, foxes, wolves, and elk. The judge agreed and ordered the couple to reduce the herd to 420. A subsequent refiling by the group cut that further to 280. Having to shift half their grazing to private land at ten times the cost plunged the Skaggses into red ink. They'd closed down and retired, were now living on a thousand dollars a month in Social Security payments.

"My family's been ranching these lands since 1834," said Bart Skaggs. "We withstood every natural disaster you can think of but we couldn't stand up to crazy radical environmentalists."

Emma Skaggs was described as *"too distraught to comment."*

When asked for his reaction to the couple's loss, ForestHaven's board member and chief complainant was unrepentant: *"The land is threatened and the land reigns supreme—above any individual's selfish needs," said Lawrence Olafson, a well-known art dealer with galleries in Santa Fe and New York City. "You can't make an omelet without breaking eggs."*

Olafson had highlighted his own comments in yellow marker.

"Proud of himself," said Darrel.

"The land reigns supreme," said Katz.

They filed the book as evidence and took it with them.

"Breaking eggs," said Two Moons as they left the house. "That bashed-in head of his."

Katz raised his eyebrows. His partner had a way with words.

They loaded the computer and its paraphernalia in the trunk of the car, and Katz warmed up the engine.

"The guy," said Two Moons. "His house has a lot of stuff, but something's missing."

"Pictures of his kids," said Katz.

"Bingo. The ex-wife I can see, but the kids? Not a single picture? So maybe they didn't like him. Doc said the scene showed lots of anger. That's how I saw it, too. What's angrier than a family thing?"

Katz nodded. "We definitely need to track down the kids. Talk to the ex, too. Want to do it before or after we find Bart and Emma Skaggs?"

"After," said Darrel. "And tomorrow. Those two got shafted. I don't feel like waking them up at"—he peered at his watch—"four-eighteen. We're well into overtime, partner."

4

Katz put on as much speed as the dark, winding roads would allow, and they made it back to the headquarters at Camino Entrada by 4:45.

After logging Olafson's computer into evidence, they did some preliminary paperwork on the case, agreed to meet for breakfast at nine at the Denny's down the block from the station, and headed home. Two Moons had the Crown Vic because this was his month for take-home, and Katz made do with his grubby little Toyota Camry. Given the state of his social life, he didn't need better wheels.

Darrel Two Moons drove to his house in the South Capital district, took off his shoes at the door, and withstood an instant of chilled feet as he unlocked the door and stepped into his living room. Nice room; he always liked coming home to it. Seeing the kiva fireplace. The old twisting vigas lining the coved ceiling. Genuine old wood, the color of molasses. Not the faux-aged logs he'd noticed at Olafson's mansion.

Who was he kidding? Olafson's place was unreal.

He took off his coat, got a raspberry Snapple from the fridge, sat down at the kitchen table, and drank.

Looking through the arch at his living room. Pictures of Kristin and the girls and him taken at the Photo Inn at the DeVargas Center last Christmas.

Just about a year ago; the girls had done some growing since.

His castle.

Right.

He loved his house, but tonight, after hiking through Olafson's spread, the place looked tiny, maybe even pathetic.

A hundred-and-eighty-grand purchase. And that had turned out to be a bargain, because South Capital was booming.

A working cop able to move into the north side courtesy of MetLife insurance and the last will and testament of Gunnery Sergeant Edward Two Moons né Montez, United States Army (ret.).

Thanks, Dad.

His eyes started to hurt, and he gulped the iced tea fast enough to bring on some brain freeze.

By now, the place had to be worth close to three hundred. An investment, for someone who could afford to sell and trade up.

A guy like Olafson could trade little houses like playing cards.

Could *have.*

Two Moons recalled Olafson's crushed skull and berated himself.

Count your blessings, stupid.

He finished the Snapple, still felt parched and got some bottled water, went into the living room, and sat with his feet up, breathing deeply to see if he could catch a hint of the soap-and-water fragrance Kristin left in her wake.

She *really* loved the house, said it was all she needed, she never wanted to move.

Fifteen hundred square feet on an eight-thousand-square-foot lot, and that was enough to make her feel like a queen. Which said a lot about Kristin.

The lot *was* nice, Darrel admitted. Plenty of room out back for the girls to play and for Kristin to plant her vegetable garden and all that other good stuff.

He'd promised to lay down some gravel pathways, hadn't followed through. Soon the ground would freeze over, and the job would have to wait until spring.

How many more d.b.'s would he encounter by then?

Soft footsteps made him look up.

"Hi, honey," said Kristin, squinting and rubbing her eyes. Her strawberry-blonde hair was ponytailed, but strands had come loose. Her pink terry-cloth robe was cinched tightly around her taut waist. "What time is it?"

"Five."

"Oh." She came over, touched his hair. She was half Irish, one-quarter Scots, the rest Minnesota Chippewa. The Indian blood expressed itself in pronounced cheekbones and almond-shaped eyes. Eyes the color of sage. Darrel had met her during a visit to the Indian Museum. She'd been working there on a summer internship, doing clerical work to pay for a painting course. The eyes had snagged him, then the rest of her had held him fast.

"A case?" she said.

"Yup." Darrel stood and hugged all five feet of her. Had to bend to do it. Dancing with Kristin sometimes nipped at his lower back. He didn't care.

"What kind of case, honey?"

"You don't want to know."

Kristin's green eyes focused. "If I didn't want to know, I wouldn't have asked."

He sat her on his lap and told her.

She said, "Did you tell Steve?"

"Tell him what?"

"That you'd had an encounter with Olafson?"

"Totally irrelevant."

Kristin was silent.

"What?" he said. "It happened a year ago."

"Eight months," she said.

"You remember?"

"I remember it was April because it was the week we were shopping for Easter."

"Eight months, a year, what's the diff?"

"I'm sure you're right, Darrel."

"Let's go to bed."

The moment she hit the mattress she popped right back to sleep, but Two Moons lay on his back and thought about the "encounter."

He'd dropped over at the Indian Museum to see a show that included a couple of Kristin's watercolors. Pictures she'd done the previous summer, sitting in the garden out back. Flowers and trees, a nice soft light. Two Moons thought it her best work, had pressed her to enter the juried show.

When she made it, his chest had swelled.

He made half a dozen visits to the show, using his lunchtime. Taking Steve twice. Steve said he loved Kristin's work.

During the fifth visit, Larry Olafson bounded in with a middle-aged couple—an all-in-black couple wearing matching nerd eyeglasses. East Coast pretentious art types. The three of them walked through the show at breakneck speed, Olafson smiling—more like sneering—when he thought no one was looking.

Uttering snide comments, too, to his too cool friends.

Darrel had seen and heard when Olafson reached Kristin's watercolors and said, "Here's exactly what I mean. Insipid as dishwater."

Two Moons felt his chest swell in another way.

He tried to cool himself down, but when Olafson and the couple headed for the exit, he found himself springing forward and blocking them. Thinking this was a bad idea, but unable to stop himself.

Like something had taken him over.

Olafson's smile faded. "Excuse me."

"Those pictures of the garden," said Darrel. "I think they're good."

Olafson stroked his white beard. "Do you, now?"

"Yeah, I do."

"Then I'm happy for you."

Two Moons didn't speak or move. The all-in-black-couple shrank back.

Larry Olafson said, "Now that we've had our erudite discussion, would you kindly get out of my way?"

"What's wrong with them?" said Two Moons. "Why'd you put them down?"

"I didn't put them down."

"That's what you did. I heard you."

"I've got a cell phone," said the woman. "I'm going to call the police."

She reached into her purse.

Two Moons stepped aside.

Olafson passed him and muttered, "Barbarian."

Darrel had felt like an idiot for weeks. Thinking about it *now* made him feel stupid.

Why had he even told Kristin?

Because he'd come home in a foul mood, ignored the girls. Ignored her.

Talk, she was always telling him. You need to learn how to *talk*.

So he'd talked. And she said, "Oh, Darrel."

"I screwed up."

She sighed. "Honey . . . forget it. It's no big deal." Then she frowned.

"What?"

"The pictures," she said. "They really *are* insipid."

He found that he'd been grinding his teeth at the memory and willed himself to relax. So he didn't like the victim. He'd worked other cases where that happened, plenty of them. Sometimes people got hurt, or worse, because they were bad or stupid.

He hadn't told Steve the story. No reason to then. No reason to now.

He'd work this one hard. For some reason, reaching that decision made him feel better.

Gunnery Sergeant Edward Montez had been all army, and Darrel, his only child, raised on bases from North Carolina to California, had been groomed to follow.

At seventeen, living in San Diego, when he found out his father was going to be sent to Germany, Darrel rebelled and went over to the nearest Marine Corps recruitment office and enlisted. Within days, he'd been assigned to basic training in Del Mar.

As his mother packed suitcases, she cried.

His father said, "It's okay, Mabel." Then he trained his black eyes on Darrel: "They're kind of extreme, but at least it's the military."

"I'll like it," said Darrel. Thinking: What the hell have I *done?*

"We'll see. Make sure you learn something from them besides killing."

"Like what?" Darrel rubbed his newly shaved head. The loss of his shoulder-length hair in ten seconds and the way it lay on the floor of a barbershop in Old Town still freaked him out.

"Like something useful," said his dad. "A trade. Unless you're planning to spend the rest of your life jumping to attention."

Midway through his hitch, his mother died. Mabel and Ed Montez were both chain-smokers, and Darrel had always worried about lung cancer. It was a heart attack that got Mom. Only forty-four, she'd been sitting in the front room of a noncom housing unit outside of Hamburg, watching *Wheel of Fortune* on U.S. Army cable, when her head pitched forward and she never moved again. Her last words: "Buy a vowel, stupid."

The Marines gave Darrel compassionate leave for a week, then he returned to the base in Oceanside. He was a lance corporal by now, training grunts, earning a rep as a tough DI. The little crying he did, he did in private.

His father quit the army and settled in Tampa, Florida, where he lived off his pension and got depressed. Half a year later, he called Darrel and announced he was moving to Santa Fe.

"Why there?"

"We're Santa Clara Indian."

"So?" Darrel had been made casually aware of his heritage. As an abstraction, something historical. The few times he'd asked his parents about it, they'd inhaled their unfiltered Camels and said, "Be proud of it, but don't let it get in the way."

Now his dad was moving *because* of it? To New Mexico? Dad had always hated the desert; when they lived in California, you couldn't get him to Palm Springs.

"Anyway," said Ed Montez, "it's time."

"For what?"

"To learn, Darrel. If I don't start learning something, I'm gonna shrivel up and die like a moth."

The next time Darrel saw his father was when he finished his Marine hitch, decided he wanted more hair on his head, and didn't re-up.

"Come out here, Darrel."

"I was thinking L.A."

"Why there?"

"Maybe go to school."

"College?" said his dad, surprised.

"Yeah."

"What you want to study?"

"Maybe computers," Darrel had lied. He hadn't a clue, knowing only that he wanted the freedom of sleeping late, meeting girls who weren't hookers or Marine groupies. He wanted to have some fun.

"Computers are good," said his dad. "The talismans of our age."

"What?"

"Talismans," said Ed Montez. "Symbols—totems."

Darrel didn't answer.

"It's complicated, Darrel. Come on out, you can go to school here. UNM's a good place, got a nice campus, and there's all sorts of scholarships for Indians."

"I like California."

"I got no one," said his dad.

When Darrel got off the plane in Albuquerque and saw the old man, he nearly fell over. Ed Montez had gone from Crew-Cut Noncom to Big Chief Whatever. His gray-streaked hair was center-parted and hung down past his shoulder blades, held in place by a beaded band.

His mop was a lot longer than Darrel's own tresses had been when his dad had ridden him about looking like "a hippie bum."

Dad's civvy clothes had changed just as radically. No more golf shirt, pressed slacks, and spit-polished oxfords. Ed Montez wore a loose-fitting linen shirt over blue jeans and moccasins.

Wore a wispy *chin* beard.

He hugged Darrel—another change—took Darrel's carry-on, and said, "I changed my name. I'm Edward Two Moons. Maybe you should think about a change."

"Genealogy," the old man explained as they made the one-hour drive to Santa Fe. So far the terrain was flat and dry, lots of empty stretches paralleling the highway, the occasional Indian casino.

Just like Palm Springs.

Seventy-five-mile-per-hour speed limit. Darrel had no problem with that. His father was doing ninety and so was everyone else.

Dad lit up and blew smoke around the cabin of the Toyota pickup. "Aren't you curious?"

"About what?"

"Genealogy."

"I know what it means. You've been looking into your roots."

"*Our* roots, son. On the drive over from Florida, I stopped in Salt Lake City, went over to the Mormon place, and did some serious studying. Found out some interesting things. Then when I got here, I did some more and it got even more interesting."

"Like what?" said Darrel, even though he wasn't sure he cared. Mostly, he was sneaking sidelong glances at the old man. Edward Two Moons? When he talked, the chin beard vibrated.

"Like our lineage goes straight back to the Santa Clara Pueblo. That's on my side. Your mom was Apache and Mohawk, but that's another story. I still got to look into that."

"Okay," said Darrel.

"Okay?"

"What do you want me to say?"

"I thought," said Ed, "that you'd be curious."

"You always said it was in the past."

"I've come to appreciate the past." His father jammed his cigarette into his mouth, reached over with his right hand, and grasped Darrel's wrist. Held on. Weird. The old man had never been one for touch.

"We're related to Maria Montez, son. Straight line all the way back to her, not a doubt."

"Who's that?"

"Maybe the greatest Indian potter ever." Ed let go, flipped his hand over. The palm was gray, coated with some kind of dust.

"This is clay, son. I've been learning the ancient art."

"You?"

"Don't be so surprised."

The closest his parents had come to art were Christmas cards taped to the walls of temporary housing.

"We move around," his mother had explained. "You put holes in the plaster, you have to patch them up. I may be dumb but I'm not stupid."

"The process is really something," his father went on. "Finding the right clay, digging it up, hand-shaping—we don't use no wheels."

We?

Darrel kept his mouth shut. They were fifteen miles out of Santa Fe, and the terrain had changed. Higher altitude, pretty mountains all around. Greener, with little pink and tan and gold houses that reflected the light. The sky was huge and blue, bluer than Darrel had ever seen. A billboard advertised duty-free gasoline at the Pojoaque Pueblo. Another one said custom adobe homes were going up in a place called Eldorado.

Not bad, but still not California.

"No wheels," his father reiterated. "The shaping's all by hand, which is pretty tough, let me tell you. Then comes the firing and it really gets complicated. Some people use a kiln, but I use an outdoor fire because the spirits are stronger outdoors. You make a wood fire, the heat's gotta be perfect. If something's wrong, everything can crack and all your work's for nothing. You want to get different colors, you use cow dung. Got to snatch it out of the fire at exactly the right time, put it back in—it's complicated."

"Sounds like it."

"Aren't you going to ask me what I make?"

"What d'you make?"

"Bears," said his dad. "And they come out pretty good. Look pretty much like bears."

"Great." Clay, dung. Outdoor spirits. His dad's hair—Jesus, it was really long. Was this some kind of dream?

"I live to make bears, Darrel. All those years I didn't do it was time wasted."

"You served your country."

Ed Montez laughed and smoked and pushed his truck to nearly a hundred.

"Dad, are you living in the pueblo?"

"I wish. Whatever land rights we got at Santa Clara are long gone. But I go out there for lessons. It's not a bad drive. I managed to hook up with Sally Montez. She's Maria's great-great-granddaughter. Great potter, won first prize at the Indian Market show two years in a row. She uses dung to get a black and red combo. Last year she got the flu, didn't have it together, so she only got honorable mention. But still, that's pretty impressive."

"Where are you living, Dad?"

"Condo. Army pension pays the rent and then some. Got myself two bedrooms, so there's plenty of room for you. Got cable 'cause the dish don't do well with all the wind."

Living with his father—his *new* father—took some getting used to.

Edward Two Moons's two-bedroom condo on the south side was more honestly described as a "one plus study." Darrel's space was an eight-by-nine room walled with bookshelves and filled by a sleeper couch that unfolded to a double bed.

Books on the shelves—that was something new. American history, Indian history. Art. Lots on art.

Incense burner in his dad's room and for a second Darrel wondered: Dope?

But the old man just liked burning incense when he read.

No ceramic bears in sight. Darrel didn't ask because he didn't want to know.

One thing was the same: His dad got up at six a.m. every day, weekends included.

No more one-handed push-ups, though. Former gunnery sergeant Ed Montez greeted each day with an hour of silent meditation. Followed by another hour of bending and stretching to one of a dozen yoga tapes.

Dad taking instructions from women in leotards.

After yoga came a long walk and a half-hour bath, fry bread and black coffee for breakfast, though by then, it was closer to lunchtime.

By two p.m., the old man was ready for his drive out to the Santa Clara Pueblo, where the cheery, corpulent Sally Montez sat in her studio out back of her spacious adobe house and fashioned gorgeous, jewel-inlaid, black-clay masterpieces. The front room of the house was a shop run by Sally's husband, Bob. He was Sally's second cousin; Sally hadn't needed to change her name.

As Sally made pots, Dad hunched at a nearby table, brow furrowed, chewing his cheek as he fashioned his bears.

Families of them, in various poses.

The first time he saw the tiny animals, Darrel thought

of Goldilocks. Then he thought: No way. They didn't even look like bears. More like pigs. Or hedgehogs. Or nothing recognizable.

Dad was no sculptor and Sally Montez knew it. But she smiled and said, "Yes, Ed, you're coming along."

She wasn't doing it for the money; Dad wasn't paying her a dime. Just because she was nice. So was Bob. And their kids. And most of the people Darrel met on the pueblo.

He started to wonder.

Dad didn't mention the name-change thing again until six months after Darrel moved in. The two of them were sitting on a bench in the Plaza, eating ice cream on a gorgeous summer day. Darrel had enrolled in UNM as a business major, gotten a 3.6 his first semester, met some girls, had some fun.

"Proud of you, son," said Ed, handing the transcript back to Darrel. "Did I ever tell you the origin of my name?"

"Your new name?"

"My only name, son. The here and now is all that counts."

His hair had grown another four inches. The old man still smoked, and his skin looked like ancient leather. But the hair was thick and youthful and glossy, even with the gray streaks. Long enough for a serious braid. Today it was braided.

"The night I decided," he said, "there were two moons in the sky. Not really, it's just the way I perceived it. 'Cause of the monsoon. I was in the condo, cooking dinner, and there was one of those monsoons—you haven't seen one yet, but you will eventually. The sky just opens up and *bam*. Sheets of rain. It can be a real dry day, bone-dry, then all of a sudden things change." He blinked, and for a second his mouth got weak. "You have arroyos turning into rushing streams. It's pretty impressive, son."

Ed licked his butter pecan cone. "Anyway, there I was cooking and the rain started coming down. I finished up, sat there wondering where life was gonna take me." Another blink. "I started thinking about your mom. I never talked much about how I felt about her, but, trust me, I *felt* about her."

He turned away, and Darrel watched some tourists file past the Indian jewelers and potters sitting in the alcove of the Palace of Governors. The Plaza across the street was filled with art kiosks and a bandstand with an open mike for amateur singers. Who said folksinging was a lost art? Or maybe that was *good* folksinging.

"Thinking about your mom made me low but also a little high. Not like in drunk. Encouraged. All of a sudden I knew I was doing the right thing by coming to this place. I'm looking out the window and the glass is all wet and all you can see of the sky is black and a big, blurry moon. Only this time, it was two moons—the wet glass bent the light in a way that created this image. Am I making myself clear?"

"Refraction," said Darrel. He'd taken Physical Science for Non-Science Majors, pulled a B.

Ed regarded his son with pride. "Exactly. Refraction. Not two totally separate moons, more like one on top of the other, maybe two-thirds overlapping. It was beautiful. And this strong feeling came over me. Your mom was communicating with me. 'Cause that's what we were like. Together all the time, but we were separate people, just enough overlap to make it work. We were fifteen when we met, had to wait until we were seventeen to get married 'cause her dad was an alcoholic hard case and he hated my guts."

"I thought Grandpa liked you."

"He *came* to like me," said Ed. "By the time you knew him, he liked everyone."

Darrel's memories of his grandfather were bland and pleasant. Alcoholic hard case? What other surprises did his father have in store?

"Anyway, the two moons were obviously your mom and me, and I decided then and there to honor her by taking the name. Consulted a lawyer here in town, went over to the courthouse, and did it. It's official and legal, son, in the eyes of the state of New Mexico. More important, it's sacred-holy in *my* eyes."

A year after Darrel moved in with his father, Edward Two Moons was diagnosed with bilateral small-cell carcinoma of the lung. The cancer had spread to his liver, and the doctors said to go home and enjoy the time he had left.

The first few months were okay, just a dry, persistent cough and some shortness of breath. Dad read a lot about the old Indian religion and seemed at peace. Darrel faked being relaxed, but his eyes hurt all the time.

The last month was rough, all of it spent at the hospital. Darrel sat by his father's bed and listened to his father breathe. Watched the monitors idly and got friendly with some nurses. No tears came, just a deep ache in his belly. He lost fifteen pounds.

But he didn't feel weak. Just the opposite, as if drawing upon some kind of reserve.

The last day of his life, Edward Two Moons slept.

Except for one time, middle of the night, when he sat up, gasping, looking scared.

Darrel rushed over and held him. Tried to ease him back down, but Dad wanted to remain upright and he fought it.

Darrel complied and his father finally relaxed. Lights from the monitors turned his face sickly green. His lips were moving, but no sound was coming out. Struggling to say something. Darrel looked him straight in the eye, but by now his father wasn't seeing anything.

Darrel held him tight and put his ear next to his father's lips.

Dry rasping came out. Then:

"Change. Son. Is. Good."

Then he sank back to sleep. An hour later, he was gone.

The day after the funeral, Darrel went over to the courthouse and filed papers for a name change.

5

Katz thought about Olafson's murder on the drive home.

Doc and Darrel had talked about anger, and maybe they were right. But if anger was the prime motivation, you'd have predicted multiple blows, not one massive crusher.

A surprised burglar would fit with that. So did the open storage room.

Some sort of confrontation, Olafson announcing he was calling the police, turning his back on the bad guy.

Stupid move. Olafson's comments about suing Bart and Emma Skaggs reeked of arrogance. Maybe he'd gotten overconfident and had not taken the burglar seriously.

The oversize chrome hammer implied the bad guy hadn't come prepared to kill. Did the selection of weapon imply some sort of symbolic deal—killed by art, like Darrel had said—or just opportunism?

Katz had lived with symbols. That's what you got when you married an artist.

A would-be artist.

First the sculptures, then the shitty paintings.

Be kind. Valerie had some talent. Just not enough.

He put her out of his mind and returned to the case. Came up with nothing new but was still thinking when he reached his space and parked and entered. The room was just as he'd left it: pin-neat. He pulled down the Murphy bed, ate, and watched TV and thought some more.

He lived in a three-hundred-square-foot tin-roofed outbuilding behind the Rolling Stone Marble and Granite Yard on South Cerillos. It had a front room and a pre-formed fiberglass lav. Warmth courtesy of a space heater, air-conditioning courtesy of opening the windows. He cooked on a hot plate, kept his few belongings in a steel locker. The view was stone slabs stacked vertically and forklifts.

Temporary lodgings that had stretched to permanent. Semipermanent, since maybe one day he'd find a real house. There was no reason to right now, because the rent was minimal and he had no one to impress. Back in New York, the same dough wouldn't have gotten him a cot in a basement.

He was the middle son of a dentist and a hygienist, the brother of two other tooth jockeys, raised in Great Neck, a onetime jock but no student, the black sheep of a res-olutely middle-class family. After dropping out of SUNY Binghamton, he'd worked as a bartender in Manhattan for five years before returning to John Jay and earning a degree in criminal justice.

During his five years with NYPD, he'd ridden a patrol car in Bed-Stuy, done some dope-undercover, some jail duty, finished up at the Two-Four in the city, working the western border of Central Park from 59th to 86th. Nice job, covering the park. Until it wasn't.

He continued to moonlight as a bartender, was socking away enough money to buy a Corvette, though he had no idea where he'd park it or when he'd use it. He was mixing ridiculous fruit martinis at a place in the Village the night he met Valerie. At first, he hadn't thought much of her. It was her girlfriend Mona who'd caught his eye; back then he'd been into breasts and blondes. Later, when he learned how crazy Mona was, he was thankful he hadn't gotten involved with her. Not that things had turned out so great with Valerie, but you couldn't put that down to her being nuts.

Just . . .

No sense lingering.

He read a paperback for a while—a police novel that bore no resemblance to any reality he knew, which was exactly what he needed. Drowsy within minutes, he placed the book on the floor, turned off the light, and stretched out.

The sun would be up soon, and by seven a.m., Al Kilcannon and the workers in the stone yard would be shouting and laughing and getting the machinery going. Sometimes Al brought his dogs and they barked like crazy. Katz had his earplugs ready on the nightstand.

But maybe he wouldn't use them. Maybe he should just get up, dress warm, and take a run, be ready to meet Darrel at Denny's.

Waking up in this dump could be depressing. He didn't miss Valerie, but he did miss greeting the morning with a warm body next to him.

Maybe he missed her a little.

Maybe he was too damned tired to know how he felt.

The night they met, Mona got picked up by some loser, and Valerie was stuck sitting there by herself. Now, out from Mona's shadow, she seemed more visible and Steve noticed her. Dark hair cut in a page, pale oval face, maybe ten extra pounds, but the distribution was pretty good. Big eyes, even from a distance. She looked forlorn and he felt sorry for her, sent her a complimentary cosmopolitan. She glanced over at the bar, raised her eyebrows, and came over.

Definitely good distribution.

They went home together to her apartment in the East Village, because she had an actual room as opposed to his curtain-partitioned space in the two-roomer on 33rd that he shared with three other guys.

The whole time, Valerie stayed forlorn, didn't talk much, but sex switched her on like a light and she made love like a tigress. Afterward, she took a joint out of her purse and smoked it down. Told him she was a sculptor and a painter, a Detroit girl, NYU degree, no gallery representation yet but she'd sold a few pieces at street fairs. He told her what his day job was, and she looked at the ashes left by the doobie and said, "You busting me?"

He laughed and revealed his own stash. Shared.

They were married three months later in an impulsive civil ceremony that proved yet another disappointment to Katz's family. Valerie's, too, as it turned out. Her dad was an attorney. She'd grown up in a borderline social set, had given her parents nothing but problems.

At first, their rebelliousness seemed enough to

cement the relationship. Soon it wasn't, and within a year they'd settled into mutual avoidance, polite asides, occasional sex of diminishing ardor. Katz was enjoying police work well enough, but he never talked about work to Valerie because talking seemed wimpy and, besides, cruelty upset her vegan soul. Also, her career was going nowhere fast, and his being content with his own job didn't seem to help.

The night things changed, he was working the latter half of a double shift, partnered with a ten-year vet named Sal Petrello. Quiet night. They'd chased a few kids who were obviously planning mischief out of the park, helped a German tourist find his way back to Fifth Avenue, investigated an assault that turned out to be a middle-aged couple bickering loudly. Ten minutes before midnight a call came in: male mental case, running around naked near Central Park West and 81st.

When they got there, they found nothing. No maniac, naked or otherwise, none of the witnesses who'd called it in, no people at all. Just darkness and foliage in the park, the sounds of traffic from the street.

"Probably a fake-o," said Petrello. "Someone screwing around."

"Probably," Katz agreed. But he wasn't sure. Something was tickling the back of his neck—so insistently that he actually reached back there to make sure no bug was exploring his skin.

No bug, just an itchy feeling.

They searched for another five minutes, came up empty, called it in as a fake-o, and started to leave.

As they made their way back to the car, Petrello said, "Better this way. Who needs lunatics?"

They'd almost made it when the guy jumped out and planted himself in front of them, blocking the pathway. Big muscular guy; square-faced and heavy-jawed, with a shaved head, pecs like sides of beef. Naked as a jaybird.

Excited, too. He howled and slashed at the air. Something shiny in his left hand. Petrello was closer to him and drew back, reached for his weapon, but not fast enough. The guy slashed again and Petrello screamed, grabbed his hand.

"Steve, he cut me!"

Katz's gun was out. The naked loony was grinning, moving toward him, stepping into filtered street light, and now Steve could see what was in his hand. Straight razor. Pearl handle. Rust-red with Petrello's blood.

Katz kept his eye on the weapon while sneaking a glance at his partner. Sal had one hand pressed tight over the wound. Blood was seeping out. Seeping, not spurting. Good, didn't look like an arterial cut.

Sal groaned. "Motherfucker. Shoot him, Steve."

The maniac advanced on Katz, waved the razor in tiny concentric arches.

Katz aimed at his face. *"Freezedon'tmove!"*

The loony looked down at his own crotch. *Real* excited.

Sal screamed, "Shoot him, Steve! I won't say nothing. Jesus, I need a Band-Aid. Would you *shoot* him, for chrissake!"

The maniac laughed. Eyes still on his erect member.

Katz said, "Put the razor down. Now."

The maniac lowered his arm, as if to comply.

Laughed in a way that curdled Katz's blood.

"Oh, God," said Sal.

He and Katz stared, unbelieving, as the crazy man

made a quick downward chopping motion and left himself minus an organ.

The department sent Katz and Petrello to shrinks. Petrello didn't mind because he was getting paid anyway, planned on taking some serious leave. Katz hated it for all sorts of reasons.

Valerie knew what had happened because it was in the *Post*. For once, she seemed to want Steve to talk, so finally he did.

She said, "Disgusting. I think we should move to New Mexico."

At first, he thought she was kidding. When he realized she wasn't, he said, "How can I do that?"

"Just do it, Steve. It's about time you were spontaneous."

"What's that supposed to mean?"

She didn't answer. They were in their apartment on West 18th, Valerie chopping salad, Katz fixing a corned beef sandwich. Cold beef. Valerie was okay with his eating meat, but she couldn't stand the smell of it cooking.

Several frosty moments later, she stopped, came over, put her arm around his waist, touched her nose to his. Withdrew, as if the gesture hadn't worked for either of them.

"Let's be honest, Steve. Things haven't been going so great between us. But I'm going to believe it's not us. It's the city sucking out our energy. All the spiritual pollution. What I need at this point in my life, Steve, is serenity, not toxicity. Santa Fe's serene. It couldn't be more different than here."

"You've been there?"

"When I was in high school. My family took a trip.

They went shopping at the Gap and Banana Republic, typical. I hit the galleries. There are tons of them there. It's a small town with great food and clubs and most of all art."

"How small?"

"Sixty thousand."

Katz laughed. "That's a block here."

"My point exactly."

"When were you thinking of doing this?"

"Sooner the better."

"Val," he said, "I'm years from a serious pension."

"Pensions are for old sick people. You've still got a chance to be young."

What did *that* mean?

"I've got to do it, Steve. I'm choking."

"Let me think about it."

"Don't think too long."

That night, after she'd gone to bed, he got on the Internet and found the Santa Fe Police Department Web site.

Dinky little department and the salary scale didn't match NYPD. Some nice things, though. Lateral transfers possible, a sixty-mile vehicle take-home policy. One opening for a detective. Lately, he'd been thinking about trying for detective, knew he'd have to wait in line at the Two-Four or any of the neighboring precincts.

Sal Petrello was telling people Katz had frozen, that it had only been luck that the loon had sliced off his own dick and not one of theirs.

He played with the computer awhile longer, pulled up some color pictures of Santa Fe. Pretty, that was for sure. No sky could be that blue, probably trick photography.

More like a village than a city.

Probably boring as hell, but what fascinating things was he doing in the big bad city anyway? He turned off the lights, got into bed, snuggled next to Valerie, put his hand on her butt, and said, "Okay, let's do it."

She grunted, removed his hand.

Most of what they owned was crap, and what they couldn't get rid of at a sidewalk sale they left behind. After packing clothing and Valerie's art supplies, they flew to Albuquerque on a warm spring day, picked up a rental car at the airport, and drove to Santa Fe.

The sky *could* be that blue.

All the space and the quiet threatened to drive Katz nuts. He kept his mouth shut. Last couple of nights he'd been dreaming about the maniac with the razor. In the dreams, not such a happy ending. Maybe he really did need to cleanse his soul.

They rented a house off St. Francis, not far from the DeVargas Center. Val went to buy art supplies, and Steve dropped in at the police department.

Teeny little place, plenty of parking out back. Relaxed pace. So *quiet.*

The chief was a woman. That might be interesting.

He picked up an application form, took it home, found Valerie all excited, emptying a bag full of paint tubes and brushes onto the folding table they ate on.

"I went back to Canyon Road," she told him. "There's an art supply store there. You'd think it would be expensive, but it's like two-thirds of what it cost me back in New York."

"Great," he said.

"Wait, I'm not finished." She inspected a tube of cadmium yellow. Smiled, put it down. "While I'm waiting I notice a check taped to the wall behind the register. Old check, the paper's yellowed. From the fifties. And guess whose it was?"

"Van Gogh."

She glared. "Georgia O'Keeffe. She used to live right there, before she bought the ranch. She bought her stuff right there, the same place I did."

Katz thought: As if that would help.

He said, "That's awesome."

She said, "Are you patronizing me, Steve?"

"No way," he insisted. "I think that's really cool."

Bad liar. Both of them knew it.

It took her three months to leave him. Ninety-four days to be exact, during which Katz got a Police Officer III job and a promise to be considered for the detective position within sixty days if no one with more experience showed up.

"I've got to be honest," he told Lieutenant Barnes. "I did undercover but no real detective work."

"Hey," said Barnes, "you spent five years in New York. I'm pretty sure you can handle the stuff we get."

On day ninety-four, he came home to find Valerie's stuff gone and a note on the folding table.

Dear Steve,

I'm sure this will be no surprise, you're no happier than me. I met someone and I want a chance to be happy. You should also be happy. Think of me as helping, not hurting you. I'll pay half of this month's rent plus utilities.

V

The someone she'd met was a guy who drove a taxi during the day and claimed to be a sculptor. That was Santa Fe, Katz had learned quickly. Everyone was creative.

Val and Taxi lasted a month, but she had no desire to come back to Katz. Instead, she embarked on a series of affairs with similar types, keeping no permanent address, painting her terrible abstractions.

A small town meant running into her all the time. The guys she was with always started off nervous about meeting Katz. Then, when they could tell he wasn't going to hit them, they relaxed and got the same sly, contented look on their faces. Katz knew what it meant; he'd experienced Val as a tigress.

He wasn't getting laid at all. Which was fine. He had no libido, was into his new job. Wearing a blue uniform that fit better than his NYPD duds, driving around and getting to know the lay of the land, enjoying the company of a series of easygoing partners, solving problems that could be solved.

Paying rent on a too big place seemed foolish, but inertia stopped him from taking the initiative to move. Then one night he got a call to check out an intruder at the Rolling Stone Marble and Granite Yard. Mostly, those were false alarms, but this time he caught some kid hiding among the slabs. No big deal, just a loser looking for a place to sniff coke. Katz arrested him and handed him over to Narco.

The owner of the yard, a big, heavy, florid man named Al Kilcannon, showed up as Katz was trundling the kid off. Heard Katz talk and said, "You from the city?"

"New York."

"Is there another city?" Kilcannon was from Astoria, Queens, had worked with some Greeks in the stone business. Ten years ago, he had moved to Santa Fe because his wife wanted peace and quiet.

"Same deal here," said Katz, sticking the kid in the back of his cruiser and slamming the door.

"She like it?"

"Last time I talked to her she did."

"Oh," said Kilcannon. "One of those—what, an artist?"

Katz smiled. "Have a good evening, sir."

"See you around, Officer Katz."

And he did, a week later, the two of them bending elbows at a bar on Water Street. Kilcannon well in his cups, but a good listener.

When Katz told him he was thinking of moving, Kilcannon said, "Hey, you know, I've got a place out back of the yard. Nothing fancy, my kid used to live there back when he was in college and hated my guts. Now he's living in Boulder and the place is empty. I'd be willing to make a trade: two hundred bucks a month, including utilities, if when you're there you watch over the place."

Katz thought about that. "What about when I'm sleeping?"

"Then you're sleeping, Steve. The main thing is someone'll be there."

"I'm still not clear what you expect me to do."

"*Be* there," said Kilcannon. "A cop being there will be a terrific deterrent. Leave your cop car where it can be seen from the street. I got big-time inventory; for me it'd be cheap insurance."

"My partner and I trade off," said Katz. "I don't get to take the car home every day."

"No sweat, Steve. When it's there, it's there. The main

thing is you'll be there and everyone'll know it. No pressure, but it could work out for both of us. It's even got cable."

Katz finished his drink. Then he said, "Sure, why not?"

Since he'd lived here, he'd caught a would-be marble thief, a real moron attempting to single-handedly make off with Kilcannon's last slab of Norwegian Rose. Nothing else, other than stray dogs and one weird situation where a coyote mom had actually made it all the way down from the Sangres and whelped a litter between two pallets of Brazilian Blue.

A good deal for him and Al, he figured. If you didn't mind living like this.

He lay on his bed, not the least bit tired. He'd coast through tomorrow on adrenaline, collapse sometime in the evening.

But he fell asleep despite himself. Thinking about Valerie. About why her name had been in Larry Olafson's Palm Pilot.

6

Breakfast was a quick affair for the two detectives. Darrel had been the one to get up early and hit the computer. He'd found a recent address for Bart and Emma Skaggs.

"Over in Embudo. Got a unit number, so they're in an apartment," he told Katz. "Far cry from running cattle."

"Embudo's pretty," said Katz.

"It's an apartment, Steve." Anger flashed in Darrel's eyes.

"You don't like our vic."

Darrel stared at him. Pushed away his plate. "Let's get going. The highway should be nice and clear by now."

Embudo was fifty miles north of Santa Fe, right where the highway meets the roiling Rio Grande. Nice little greenbelt town, really more like an oasis in the high desert. Even when the drought was heavy, the river kept the environs lush and moist.

The Skaggs residence was a room over a garage out back of a roadside shop that sold vintage clothing and chilis and pickled vegetables and yoga tapes. The owner was a spaced-out white-haired woman in her fifties with some kind of middle European accent who said, "They clean for me and I give them a deal on the rent. Nice people. Why are you here?"

"We like nice people," said Two Moons.

Katz examined a packet of chili spices. Blue ribbon prize at last year's show.

"They're good," said the white-haired woman. She wore black yoga pants and a red silk blouse and twenty pounds of amber jewelry.

Katz smiled at her and put the packet down and hurried after Two Moons.

"Police?" Emma Skaggs opened the door and emitted a sigh. "Come in, I think we can find some room for you."

The place was no bigger than Katz's shack, with the same space heater, hot-plate setup, and a bathroom in the back. But the lower ceilings and tiny windows cut into what looked to be real adobe walls gave it a prison-cell feel. Some attempt had been made to warm it up: worn pillows on an old clumsy Victorian sofa, dog-eared paperbacks in a cheap bookcase, threadbare but nicely dyed Navajo rugs flung across the stone floor, a few pieces of Pueblo pottery on the kitchenette counter.

A photo over the bricked-up fireplace showed scrawny-looking cows grazing in a yellow meadow.

A toilet flushed in the rear bathroom, but the door stayed closed.

Emma Skaggs cleared newspapers off two folding chairs and motioned the two detectives to sit. She was a short, lean, sun-whipped woman who looked her age, with dyed-red hair and wrinkles deep enough to hide gemstones. Blue jeans stretched over hard hips and a knitted wool sweater. It was cold inside. Her chest was flat. Her eyes were gray.

"You're here about Olafson," she said.

Katz said, "You heard."

"I watch TV, Detective. And if you think you're going to learn anything valuable here, you're wasting your time."

"You had conflict with him," said Darrel.

"No," said Emma Skaggs. "He had conflict with us. We were doing fine until that bastard came along."

"No love lost."

"Not a flicker. Want some coffee?"

"No, thanks, ma'am."

"Well, I'm gonna get some." Emma made the two-stride journey to the kitchenette and poured herself a cup of black. Dishes were stacked in a drainer, cans and bottles and canisters were ordered neatly, but still the place was cluttered. Too much stuff for too little room.

The bathroom door swung open, and Bart Skaggs came out drying his hands. Bandy-legged and broad with a potbelly that hung over his rodeo buckle. He wasn't much taller than his wife, with the same broiled, burnished look to his skin that comes from decades of UV abuse.

No doubt he'd heard the detectives' voices, because he registered no surprise.

"Coffee?" said Emma.

"Yeah, sure." Bart Skaggs came over, offered a sand-paper left hand, remained on his feet. A bandage was wrapped across his right hand. Swollen fingers extended from the gauze.

"I was telling them," said Emma, "that they wouldn't learn anything from us."

Bart nodded.

Two Moons said, "Your wife says life was going along okay until Olafson came along."

"Him and the others." Bart Skaggs's tongue rolled around in his cheek, as if dislodging a tobacco plug.

"The others meaning ForestHaven."

"ForestHell is more like it," said Emma. "Buncha do-gooders wouldn't last two hours in the forest if you dropped them there without their cell phones. And he was the worst."

"Olafson."

"Until he came along, they were mostly talk. Then all of a sudden we're getting court papers." Her skin took on a rosy hue and gray eyes turned stormy. "It was so wrong that the poor kid who served us apologized."

Bart Skaggs nodded again. Emma handed him a cup. He bent a knee, flexed a leg, drank. Over the rim, his eyes appraised the detectives.

Emma said, "If you came here expecting us to lie about being all choked up, you wasted your time."

"We do a lot of that," said Katz.

"Bet you do," said Emma. "But *we* didn't used to. Back when we were allowed to work an honest day. We stayed busy every minute, and it wasn't 'cause of no plans to get rich—you don't get rich running beef. Any idea what they're paying on the hoof nowadays? All those vegetarians lying about good, healthy meat."

Yet another nod from her husband. Strong, silent type?

"But still," she went on, "we liked it. It was what our

families did for generations. Who were we hurting, grazing down weeds and plants that needed to be trimmed anyway for fire risk? Like the elk don't do the exact same thing? Like the elk don't deposit their manure right in the streams? That's something we never did, no matter what anyone says."

"What's that?" said Darrel.

"Pollute the water. We made sure the herd always did its business away from the water. We respected the land, a lot more than any do-gooder. You want your healthy environment? I'll give you your healthy environment: ranching. Animals doing what they're supposed to be doing, *where* they're supposed to be doing it. Everything in its place: That's the way God intended it."

Katz said, "Larry Olafson ended all that."

"We tried to talk to him—to be logical. Didn't we, Barton?"

"Yup."

"I telephoned him personally," she went on. "After we got the court papers. He wouldn't even take my call. Had some snotty young snip answering the phone who went on like a broken record. 'Mr. Olafson is occupied.' That was the whole point. *We* wanted to be occupied with our God-given jobs. *He* had other plans."

"You ever reach him?" said Two Moons.

"I had to drive over to Santa Fe, find that art gallery of his."

"When was this?"

"Couple of months ago, who remembers?" She snorted. "If you call that art. Occupied? He was hanging around, drinking foamy coffee. I introduced myself and told him he was making a big mistake, we weren't the land's enemy or his or anyone's, all we wanted to do was bring our beef to market, all we needed was a few more years and then we'd probably retire, so could he please lay off."

Katz said, "Were you really planning on retiring?"

She sagged. "No choice. We're the last generation interested in ranching."

Katz nodded sympathetically. "Kids have their own ideas."

"Ours sure does. Kid, singular. Bart Junior. He's an accountant over in Chicago, went to school at Northwestern and stayed there."

"He does good," said Bart. "He don't like getting dirty."

"Never did," said Emma. "Which is fine." Her expression said it wasn't.

"So," said Two Moons, "you told Olafson you needed a few more years before retirement. What did he say?"

"He gave me this look. Like I was a slow child. Said, 'None of that is *my* concern, *dear.* I'm speaking for the *land.*'" Emma's voice had dropped to a baritone parody— the snooty voice of a sitcom butler. Her hands were balled into fists.

"He didn't want to listen," said Katz.

"Like he was God," said Emma. "Like someone died and *made* him God."

"Now he's the one who died," said Bart. Pronouncing the words quietly but distinctly. It was the closest he'd come to an independent statement since the detectives had arrived. They turned to him.

"Any ideas about that, sir?" Two Moons asked.

"About what?"

"Mr. Olafson's death."

"A good thing," said Bart. "Not a bad thing at all." He sipped coffee.

Darrel said, "What happened to your hand, Mr. Skaggs?"

"He got ripped by barbed wire," said Emma. "We had some old rolls of it left over and he was trucking them off to the surplus dealer and he slipped and the edge caught his hand. Big rolls. I told him it was a two-person job, not a one-person job, but as usual he didn't listen. He's a stubborn one."

"Like you isn't?" Bart snapped back.

Two Moons said, "When did this happen?"

"Four days ago," Bart answered. "Never ended up taking the wire to surplus."

"Sounds painful."

Bart shrugged.

The detectives let the room go silent.

"You're making a mistake if you're thinking he had anything to do with it." Emma shook her head. "Bart never done a cruel thing in his life. Even when he slaughters an animal, he does it with kindness."

Katz said, "How do you do that, Mr. Skaggs?"

"Do what?"

"Slaughter with kindness."

"Shoot 'em," said Skaggs. "Right here." Reaching behind his neck, he fingered the soft spot where stalk met skull. "Shoot 'em at an upward angle. You wanna get 'em in the medulla oblongata."

"Not a shotgun, right?" said Katz. "Too messy from up close."

Bart looked at him as if he were a space alien. "You use a long gun or a large-caliber handgun with a Magnum load."

Emma stepped in front of her husband. "Let's be clear: We never did any big-time slaughtering. That woulda been against regulations. We ship the cattle to a processing plant in Iowa, and they do everything from there. I was talking when we needed meat for our own table. I'd tell him, and he'd run an old steer into the pen and put it out of its misery. We never took the good beef for ourselves. But even with tired old beef, you dry-age it a couple of days in the refrigerator, then you marinate it, in beer or something, and you got yourself a tasty steak."

Bart Skaggs stretched his free arm. The gauze bandage had yellowed around the edges and was dotted with blood. "Jewish rabbis use the knife across the throat. I seen 'em do that over in Iowa. If you're good with the knife and the knife's real sharp, it's fast. Those rabbis cut good. They don't even stun 'em. If you're not good, it's messy."

"You stun 'em," said Katz.

"Just in case."

"Before you shoot 'em."

"Yup. To quiet 'em down."

"How do you go about it?"

"You distract 'em by talking to 'em, nice and low and comforting. Then you hit 'em upside the head."

"The medulla?"

Bart shook his head. "In front, over the eyes. To con-fuse 'em."

"Hit 'em with what?" said Katz.

"A bar," said Bart. "A sledgehammer. I had a piece of axle from an old truck. That worked good."

"I'm trying to picture it," said Katz. "First you hit 'em

from the front, then you run around and shoot 'em from the back?"

The room fell silent.

"Am I missing something?" said Katz.

Emma turned stony. "I see where all this is leading, and you're really wasting your time."

Suddenly, her husband took hold of her arm and drew her back so that she was no longer blocking him. She started to speak but thought better of it.

Bart fixed his eyes on Katz's. "If you're doing the shooting, you're not doing the stunning. Someone else stuns 'em, and when their legs buckle, you shoot 'em. Otherwise, the animal goes skittish and it can jump and you miss. That happens, you have to shoot 'em a bunch of times and it's real messy."

For him a long speech. Warming to the topic.

"Sounds like a two-person job," Two Moons stated evenly.

More silence.

"Yup," Bart finally said.

"We used to do it together," said Emma. "I used the hammer and Bart used the gun. Same way we did everything back when we were ranching. Teamwork. That's what it takes. That's why we got a good marriage."

"Cows are big animals," said Darrel. "To get leverage you'd need to stand on top of something, right?"

"Why's all this important?" said Emma.

"Call us curious, ma'am."

She glared.

Katz said, "Do you stand on a ladder, Mr. Skaggs?"

"The animal's in a pen," said Bart. "Tight so it can't move around too much. The way we had it at the ranch, the pen was dug out lower than the rest of the yard. You'd walk 'em down a ramp to get in there. And then we used benches on top of that so we were tall enough."

A small man feeling big as he slaughtered, thought Katz.

"It ain't rocket science." Emma glared at them. "You oughta be ashamed of yourselves . . . making two old-timers like us feel like criminals."

Two Moons shrugged. "All I'm saying is I'd be pretty sore at Olafson. The man took bread out of your mouths."

"He did worse than that. He took bread out and *burned* it. Knowing we were barely treading water and making sure we drowned." She waved an arm around the cramped, close room. "Think this is the way we want to live? The man's dead and gone. True, I'm not shedding any tears. But we sure as heck didn't harm a hair on his head. With him dead or alive we're no better off. The court says we can't run the herd, end of story."

"Like you said," Two Moons countered, "before Olafson joined the group, they were all talk. With him gone, couldn't you go back to court?"

"With whose money?" She peered at Darrel. "You're an Indian, right? I got Choctaw in me, from way back. Maybe that's why I loved working the land. You should understand what I'm talking about. That man accused us of raping the land, but *he* raped *us*."

"Revenge can be sweet," said Katz.

"Don't be an idiot!" Emma snapped. "Why would I ruin my life for *him*? I got my health and so does Barton." Her smile was sudden. Vaguely poisonous. "Besides, I got a check from the U.S. government, rolls in every month whether I lie around in bed or get up. That's heaven, right? That's your promised land."

The couple took the detectives outside, over to a storage shed behind the garage that looked ready to collapse. Freezing inside, the chill from the ground going right through your shoes. Bart showed the detectives the offending barbed-wire roll, along with other junk, including a towing winch. Big, heavy thing, rusted at some of the points. If there was blood there, the detectives couldn't see it.

Without warning, Bart unwound the gauze on his hand and showed them the jagged gash, two or so inches long, that ran from the webbing between his thumb and his forefinger down to his knobby wrist.

It had been stitched together with the thickest surgical thread Katz had ever seen. The edges of the cut had begun to scab, there was some leakage around the sutures, and the skin had gone puffy and inflamed. It looked to be a few days old.

Katz asked the name of the doctor who'd done the sewing.

Emma Skaggs laughed.

Bart said, "You're looking at her."

"You, Mrs. Skaggs?"

"None other."

"Are you trained as a nurse?"

"Trained as a wife," said Emma. "Been patching him up for forty years."

Bart grinned and brandished the wound.

Emma said, "I got veterinary needles and thread left over from the ranch. For him you need it, the big-gauge stuff. He's got the hide of a bull. Got vet antibiotics, too.

Same stuff they make for humans, only for animals it's a whole lot cheaper."

"What'd you use for anesthesia?" said Katz. "On the other hand, maybe I don't want to know."

"Crown Royal, ninety proof." Bart broke into loud guffaws. It took him a moment to settle down. "You fellows seen enough?" He started rewrapping the hand.

Darrel said, "Looks to be a little infected."

"*Little*'s the key word," said Emma. "You can't get hurt by a little of anything."

"Unlike Mr. Olafson," said Katz. "Know of anyone else who resented him?"

"Nope," said Emma, "but if he treated others like he treated us, there had to be plenty more out there."

Katz said, "Would you mind if we made an appointment for a print tech to come by to get both your fingerprints?"

"Wouldn't mind a'tall," Bart said.

"Treating us like criminals," Emma muttered.

"It's routine," Two Moons answered.

"His got to be on file, somewhere," said Emma. "From when he served in Korea. Mine aren't, but suit yourselves. Must be nice to have all that free time."

Darrel said, "Meanwhile, it would be good if you folks don't take any long road trips or the like."

"Sure," said Emma. "We were just about to fly off to El Morocco, or wherever it is." She turned to her husband. "That place where they gamble and wear monkey suits, like from the James Bond movies?"

"Monaco," said Bart. "Sean Connery plays baccarat there."

"There you go," she said. To the detectives: "He was always one for the movies."

• • •

On the drive back, Katz said, "Pour some whiskey down my gullet, Maw, and stitch away."

"You like 'em for the murder?"

"They hated him enough and they know how to deliver a good head smack, but if Ruiz is right about the angle of impact, they're too short."

"Maybe they brought a ladder." Even Darrel smiled at the thought.

"And funny little clown shoes and a flower that spurts water," said Katz. "If they were going to be that prepared, they'd have brought a weapon. The use of a pickup weapon says maybe it wasn't premeditated. I guess art galleries do keep ladders around, for hanging pictures high, so theoretically there could've been one already out. Except the walls of Olafson's place aren't that high, and the idea of either of them scrambling up on a ladder to bop Olafson sounds pretty ridiculous."

"You're right," said Darrel. "If those two wanted him dead, they'd have come ready to do it. What about the son?"

"The accountant in Chicago? Why him?"

"He didn't like getting his own hands dirty, but he could've felt real bad about Mom and Pop losing the ranch. Maybe he figured as a white-collar guy he could have a one-on-one with Olafson. What if he flew out to meet with Olafson and Olafson treated him the way he'd treated Mom? One thing led to another, Olafson blew him off, walked away from him in that arrogant way of his, and Bart Junior lost it."

That arrogant way of his. Like Darrel knew something Katz didn't. Katz said, "Insult someone's mother and you never know. Let's check the son out."

7

They hit a traffic snag just outside the city limits and made it back to the station at 1:45 p.m. The drive from Embudo back to Santa Fe had taken them past the turnoff for the Santa Clara Pueblo, but Two Moons didn't seem to notice.

Not that he was likely to mention it. The one time Katz had tried to talk about his partner's Indian roots, Darrel had changed the subject. The next day, though, he'd brought in a tiny ceramic bear. Kind of crude but the animal did have a cute look.

"What my father did during the last months of his life," Two Moons explained. "He made about five hundred of 'em, stored 'em in boxes. After he died, his pottery teacher gave them to me. She said he wasn't proud of 'em, that he had wanted to wait until he mastered the art to show all his work to me. That my approval had been important to him. She figured I should have them. You can keep it if you want."

"It's nice," Katz had said. "You sure, Darrel?"

"Yeah, it's fine." Two Moons had shrugged. "I gave a few to my girls, but how many do they need? If you know any other kids, I got plenty more."

Since then, the bear had kept Katz company while he cooked, more like warmed stuff up. It sat next to his hot plate. What it symbolized, he really didn't know, but he supposed it had something to do with strength.

The two detectives grabbed sandwiches from a station vending machine and plugged Barton Skaggs Jr. into the databases.

No criminal record but the accountant did merit a couple of Google hits. Junior was listed as a partner in a big Chicago firm, and last summer he had given a talk on tax shelters. After some fiddling with the reverse directories, they found his residence—an address on the North Shore of the Loop, not far from Michigan Avenue.

"That's a nice neighborhood," said Katz. "Right on the water, I think."

"Crunching numbers beats running cattle," said Two Moons. "Let's give him a call."

They reached Skaggs at his accounting firm. An articulate, educated-sounding man, any traces of his upbringing long gone. On the surface, he appeared to have nothing in common with his parents, but as he talked, he got increasingly assertive and the detectives heard nuances of his mother's stridency.

"I'm astonished that you'd even consider Mom and Dad in that context."

"We don't, sir," said Katz. "We're just making inquiries."

"Isn't one persecution enough? They were destroyed

financially and emotionally, and now you suspect them of something that horrible? Unbelievable. You'd be well advised to focus your efforts elsewhere."

"When's the last time you've been out to Santa Fe, Mr. Skaggs?"

"Me? Last Christmas. Why?"

"So you haven't been in regular contact with your parents."

"I certainly *am* in regular contact. We talk regularly."

"But no visits out here?"

"I just told you, last Christmas. We spent a week—I brought my family. Now, why is that—"

"I'm just wondering," said Katz, "if you ever met Lawrence Olafson."

Several beats passed before Barton Skaggs Jr. said, "Never. Why would I?" He laughed harshly. "This has to be the most inane conversation I've had in a long time. And I do believe I'm going to terminate it right now."

"Sir," said Darrel, "I'm kind of curious about one thing. Your folks were destroyed financially. From what I saw, they're living pretty down-and-out. Now, you, on the other hand—"

"Make a lot of money," Junior snapped. "Live on the North Shore. Drive a Mercedes. Send my kids to private school. You think I haven't tried to help them? I even offered to bring them out here, set them up in a nice condo, all expenses paid, though Lord only knows how they'd handle the city. I would've bought them a new place anywhere in New Mexico, somewhere they could keep some animals and left-wing lunatics wouldn't harass them. They refused."

"Why?"

"*Why?*" Junior sounded incredulous. "You've met

them. Surely you can't be that . . . that imperceptive. Why do you think? They've got pride. They're stubborn. Or maybe it's just plain old stick-in-the-mud inertia. They're the parents, I'm the kid, they raised me, ergo, I take from them. It can't be the other way around. Now, for God's sake, leave them alone. Let them *be*."

The detectives spent the next couple of hours trying to learn if Barton Skaggs Jr. had made any recent trips to Santa Fe. The task was a lot harder post–September 11; airlines were skittish, so their inquiries got mired down in gobs of red tape. Being transferred from department to department, getting hot ear from the phone's receiver. In the end, Katz and Two Moons came away pretty well convinced Skaggs hadn't flown from Chicago to Albuquerque or from any other Midwest city to any other New Mexico city. Nor had he taken any private flights directly to the Santa Fe airport. None of the major hotels had his name on their ledgers.

"I believe him," Two Moons announced.

"Hey," said Katz, "maybe he drove out West in the Mercedes. Living in his car. All that leather would make for cushy digs."

"Don't think so."

"Why not?" Katz asked.

"Just don't think so."

"Some spirit talking to you, Darrel?"

"More like I don't see him leaving his job and family to barrel down to Santa Fe to whack Olafson. And why now? None of that makes any sense. There's gotta be a better explanation."

"So you tell me," Katz said.

"I would if I knew." Two Moons scratched his head. "Now what?"

Katz scratched his head, too. The mannerism was catching. He said, "Let's call Doc and see if he's done the autopsy."

Ruiz had finished the postmortem, but he had nothing new to tell them.

"Everything fits with my initial hypothesis. One massive, crushing blow to the skull—you can see where the bone got driven right into the brain—did all sorts of damage."

"You're still thinking about the perp being a tall bad guy?" said Two Moons.

"Or a short bad guy on stilts."

"What about the tox screen?"

"The fancy stuff hasn't come in yet, but I can tell you there was no dope or alcohol in Olafson's system."

"Clean living," said Katz.

"At least recently," said Dr. Ruiz. "There was some old cirrhotic scarring of the liver, indicating serious alcohol usage in the past."

"Reformed drunk."

"Or just a guy who'd decided to moderate."

"So much for good intentions," said Two Moons.

Darrel called his wife. Katz phoned the gallery. Summer Riley answered.

"Have you learned anything?" she said.

"Not yet, Ms. Riley. Any art missing?"

"I just started going through the inventory. Nothing so far, but there's tons of unframed canvases back here."

"Did Mr. Olafson ever talk about having a drinking problem in the past?"

"Sure," said Summer. "He was open about it. Like he was about everything."

"What did he tell you?"

"We would go out to lunch and I'd order a glass of wine. Larry would look at it kind of . . . longingly, know what I mean? But he ordered club soda. He told me he had done some serious drinking when he was younger, that it was one of the reasons his marriage broke up. He said he'd been lucky to get help."

"Where?"

"Some sort of spiritual counselor."

"Back in New York?"

"Exactly," she said. "A long time ago."

"Do you know the name of Mr. Olafson's ex-wife?"

"Chantal. She's Chantal Groobman now. As in Robert Groobman." Silence over the line. "Groobman and Associates? Investment banking? He's *huge*!"

Such enthusiasm, proving what Katz always suspected. That size really does matter.

A woman with an English accent answered at the Groobman apartment on Park Avenue. From the address, Katz knew exactly where it was: between 73rd and 74th. He visualized ten rooms with high ceilings, a snooty uniformed maid inside and a snooty uniformed doorman out front. For a moment, he experienced a pang of longing.

"Mrs. Groobman?"

"This is Alicia Small, her personal assistant."

Katz introduced himself, attempting to make some

New York small talk. It was the wrong move. Alicia Small was in no mood for chumminess and she turned frosty. "Mrs. Groobman is indisposed."

"Any idea when she'll be unindisposed?"

"None. I'll forward your message."

"Forward?" said Katz. "Does that mean she's out of the city?"

Pause. "She's in the city. Leave your number and I'll inform her—"

"Are you aware that her ex-husband has been murdered?"

"I'm quite aware," said Alicia Small.

"How long have you been working for 'Madame'?"

"Three years. If that's all, Mr. Katz—"

"It's *Detective* Katz."

"Excuse. *Detective* Katz. Now, if we're through—"

"Actually we're not. I need the names of Mr. Olafson's children."

"I'm not at liberty to discuss family."

"It's public knowledge." Katz didn't bother to keep the annoyance out of his voice. "Why make my life difficult?"

"How do I know you're who you say you are?"

"Here's my number at the Santa Fe Police Department. Call and check me out, but don't take too long."

It was an offer most people refused. Alicia Small said, "Recite those numbers again, please."

The second time around, she was just as cool but resigned. "What would you like to know?"

"The names of my victim's children."

"Tristan and Sebastian Olafson."

"How old are they?"

"Tristan's twenty and Sebastian's twenty-three."

"And where might they be found?"

"Mr. Katz, I'm just not comfortable—"

"Detective—"

"Yes, yes, Detective Katz."

She was peeved, but so was he. "Ms. Small, your comfort isn't high priority. I need to talk to the boys."

A sigh floated through the receiver. "Tristan's at Brown University and Sebastian's traveling in Europe."

"Where in Europe?"

"Italy."

"Where in Italy?"

"Venice."

"Where in Venice?"

"The last time I heard he was staying at the Danieli Hotel."

"Vacation?"

"He's studying at the Peggy Guggenheim."

"Art historian?"

"He paints," said Alicia Small. "Good evening, *Mister* Katz."

They split up the Olafson boys. Katz located Tristan in his dorm room at Brown. The boy had the deep voice of a man and had learned about his father's death from his mother.

"Do you have any clues?" he asked Katz. "About who did it?"

"Not yet. Do you?"

"Could be anyone. He wasn't well liked."

"Why's that?"

"He wasn't a nice person." A cynical laugh. "If you did an ounce of investigating, you'd know that."

Katz ignored the barb and tried to get more out of him, but the boy had nothing more to say. He seemed unmoved by losing his parent. When Katz hung up, he realized Tristan had never referred to Olafson as anything other than "he."

Two Moons told Katz that he had located Sebastian Olafson. He'd been sleeping in his room at the Danieli.

"Kid was pissed. Not just because I woke him up. More like I was bugging him, asking questions about Olafson. He said his dad was a nasty man."

"Same from the other son."

"Close-knit family."

"Popular victim," said Katz. "This is going to be a barrel of laughs."

At seven p.m., they were ready to pack it in. As they were putting on their jackets, Katz's desk phone rang. Chantal Groobman was returning his call and leaving a message. Astonished, Katz raced back to his desk. He and Darrel picked up their extensions simultaneously.

"This is Detective Steve Katz. Thank you, ma'am, for getting back so promptly."

"How can I help you, Detective Katz?"

She was a pleasant-sounding woman, with a light, friendly voice. After being snobbed out by her personal assistant, he'd expected to be stonewalled.

"Whatever you can tell us about your ex-husband would be helpful, ma'am."

"Poor Larry," she said. "He could be well intentioned, but he had a knack for making people angry. I do believe part of that was attention-seeking behavior. The rest was strategy. Back when Larry began his business, he learned that art makes people, even wealthy people, insecure. He became adept at subtle intimidation. He found that a certain degree of calculated obnoxiousness could help propel his career."

"Art buyers like to be mistreated?" said Katz.

"Some do, some don't. The key is knowing who to abuse and who to pander to. Larry was good at it. But sometimes even the finest dancer missteps. Do you have any suspects?"

"Not yet."

"Poor Larry," she repeated. "He really thought he was immortal."

"If you don't mind my asking, ma'am, was Mr. Olafson's abrasive behavior the reason you divorced him?"

"I'm sure that was part of it," said Chantal Groobman. "But the main reason was Larry and I both discovered that he was confused."

"About?"

"Take a wild guess, Detective Katz."

A throaty laugh. *Like Valerie in her tigress mode.* Katz said, "His sexuality."

"Correct. You have a New York accent. Are you from here?"

"Yes, ma'am."

"We New Yorkers are so astute."

"So," said Katz, "Mr. Olafson came out of the closet?"

"When I knew him, he was groping to find his *inner* self. You'd be in a better position to tell me the final disposition of his love life. I haven't seen Larry in years. Neither have my sons. I know you contacted them and I suppose that was necessary. But I do wish you'd leave them alone. They're very upset by Larry's death."

"Ma'am," said Katz, "with all due respect, they didn't sound very upset."

"You don't know them, Detective Katz. I'm their mother."

"How'd they get along with their dad?"

"They despised him. When they were small, Larry ignored them. When they entered adolescence, he gave them a bit more attention in the form of acid criticism. Larry could be quite cutting. In any event, the lack of a paternal bond had nothing to do with Larry's death. Yesterday, Tristan was taking finals at Brown, and I'm prepared to supply any number of written affidavits to that effect. Similarly, Sebastian was working at the Guggenheim, just as he has been for four months, in full view of the staff there."

"You've done your homework, Mrs. Groobman."

"A parent—a real parent—does that."

"When did Mr. Olafson's sexual confusion emerge?"

"He was always confused, Detective. *I* was too foolish to notice it. The problem began when *Larry* noticed it."

"Is that when the drinking started?"

"Ah," she said. "So you know about that. Did Larry lapse?"

"The autopsy revealed old scarring on his liver."

"Oh," said Chantal Groobman. "How . . . sad." Her voice actually broke between the two words.

"Mr. Olafson told friends he'd received help from a spiritual counselor."

"Is that what he called it?" she said. "I never saw Dr. Weems as particularly spiritual. More of a religious . . . athletic coach."

The name was familiar to Katz, but he couldn't remember why. "What kind of a doctor was he?"

"I don't think I ever knew. Larry didn't say and I didn't ask."

Then it came to Katz: the painting in Olafson's house. Little kids dancing around the maypole. The signature: *Michael Weems.* He said, "Could it be that Dr. Weems was seeking another connection with your ex?"

"What do you mean? Sexual?" She laughed. "I don't think so."

"More like representation. He being the artist and your husband being the art dealer."

"Weems an artist?" Again the laugh. "You're kidding! That, I find impossible to believe."

"Why, ma'am?"

"Myron Weems was the last person I'd predict would go artsy."

"I meant Michael Weems," said Katz.

"Ah . . . but of course. Now I understand your confusion. Yes, Michael Weems is a painter of serious repute. She's also a woman, Detective. Myron was her husband."

"Was?"

"Yet another marital bond rent asunder. Despite Myron's alleged spirituality."

"An artist and a minister. Kind of an interesting match."

"They're from Nebraska," she said. "Or some other flat place. Corn-fed, salt-of-the-earth people. Both went to Bible school. Michael had talent and came to New York because where else does talent gravitate? Her rise was pretty rapid—she is a first-rate artist. Myron tagged along and attempted to climb socially."

"Spiritual adviser to the art world?" said Katz.

"Something like that. Then he decided he didn't like

that world, they divorced, and he returned to Nebraska. Or wherever it was."

"Not before helping Mr. Olafson."

"If that's what Larry told people, then I'm sure that's what happened. Now, I really do have to go, Detective. I'm already late for a function."

Click.

Katz had a few more questions, but when he called her back, the phone rang and no message machine switched on.

Katz and Two Moons made a second attempt to leave, got as far as the stairs down to the ground floor when Bobby Boatwright called out, "Hey!" from down the hall.

He'd gotten into Olafson's computer and he gave them a rundown.

"No big security measures or attempt to conceal. The guy used 'Olafsonart' as his password. Nothing much to hide, either. He bookmarked several art-pricing sites and the major auction houses, some porno, most of it gay, some of it straight, and a bunch of restaurant guides locally as well as in New York. He's got a brokerage account at Merrill Lynch, stocks and bonds, a little over two million bucks. From what I can tell, the account has dropped from where it was during the tech boom, but it's up from the low."

"What about all his business finances?" asked Two Moons.

"Not in the computer," said Bobby. "Try his accountant."

It was eight p.m., too late to call anyone. They'd really learned nothing. Soon the brass all the way up to the chief would be asking questions. Two Moons knew it would generate lots of column space in the *Santa Fe New Mexican*—the local daily that had as big a sports section as it did a front section. (When his father told him that the local team was called the Isotopes, Darrel was sure the old man was putting him on.) This kind of high-profile case would even be star material for the *Albuquerque Journal*. He hoped the girls wouldn't be bothered by it. All of their friends knew what Dad did for a living.

They stepped out into the cold night air and walked to their vehicles.

Darrel said, "Something you should know. I had . . . I don't know what you'd call it. An altercation, I guess. With Olafson."

"That so?" said Katz.

"Yeah." Two Moons told him the story.

Katz said, "I would've been pissed off, too."

"Yeah, well, I thought you should know."

Katz smiled. "Doesn't seem relevant, chief. Unless you killed him."

"If I killed him, there'd be no body to find."

"Funny, partner." A pause. "Actually, I was thinking the same thing."

Two Moons allowed himself a tiny smile.

They walked a few more steps before Katz said, "As long as we're confessing, here's mine: Valerie's name showed up in Olafson's Palm Pilot."

"She's an artist," said Darrel. "I guess there'd be a logical reason."

"She *thinks* she's an artist, Darrel. You've seen her stuff."

"True."

"In fact," Katz went on, "lately, from the way she's

been talking, I don't even think *she* believes it anymore. Olafson was high-end. There's no way he would have considered representing her."

"So there's another reason for her being in his directory," said Darrel.

"Exactly." Katz sighed. "I thought I'd go over and talk to her about it. I was gonna do it first, then tell you. Because I can't see it turning out to be anything important."

"Makes sense."

"I don't want you to think I was holding back or anything like that."

"I don't think that."

"Good," said Katz. "I was gonna let it sit until tomorrow, but I think I'll go over and see her now. We could both go."

Two Moons said, "If you don't mind, I'd like to get home."

"No problem, Darrel. I can do it alone."

"Yeah, it would be better that way."

8

Sitting in his Toyota, with the engine idling and the heat blowing, Katz tried Valerie's home number. Her machine switched on, and nobody interrupted when he left his name. He then drove to the Plaza, parked on the lower level of the municipal lot near the La Fonda hotel, and walked over to the Sarah Levy Gallery. The sign on the door said *Closed,* but the place was all windows, and with the lights on, he could see Sarah sitting behind her desk, surrounded by gorgeous black-on-black pottery from San Ildefonso and a grouping of gaping-mouth story-tellers from the Cochiti Pueblo. Reading spectacles were perched on her nose. Katz rapped lightly on the door-jamb. Sarah looked up over her glasses, smiled, came over, and unlocked the door.

"Steve."

"Working late, Sarah?"

"Always." Santa Fe's premium dealer in Pueblo ceramics was fifty-five, rail-thin, and glamorous, with a

sheet of blue-white hair hanging down to her shapely buttocks and a heart-shaped face that needed no makeup.
Her husband was a plastic surgeon, and rumor had it
she'd made use of his services. Katz knew it to be a lie.
Sarah had naturally young skin.

"Val around?"

"Not here, but you know where." She glanced up the
block.

"Okay, thanks."

"Sure, Steve." She touched his sleeve. "When she left,
she was in a good mood."

Warning him he might be intruding.

"I'll try not to ruin it."

The Parrot Bar was a short walk away, on San Francisco Street, between a fossil shop and a place that sold
only white clothing. A Doobie Brothers cover band was
playing tonight, and bass thumps poured out to the sidewalk. *Oh, oh, oh . . . listen to the music.* Out on the curb to
the right of the entry, three bikers were drinking beer.
Illegal, and most everyone knew Katz was a cop. They also
knew he couldn't have cared less. The bikers greeted him
by name, and he gave a small salute in return.

He made his way through a throng of drinkers and
shimmying dancers, up to the overly lacquered bar where
Val was sure to be.

And there she was on a center stool wearing a black
halter and blue jeans and boots. Sandwiched between two
ponytailed guys with hunched backs. The old shearling
she wore during the winter had fallen from her lap and
lay on the floor, getting trampled.

Ponytail on the left had gray hair and a skimpy beard.
His hand rested on Val's bare back, partially covering the

gladiolus tattoo she'd gotten last summer. Right-Side Pony's gut hung over his belt. His stubby fingers caressed Val's butt, but she didn't seem to notice.

Wide butt, Katz noted. The ten extra pounds had stretched to twenty. Still distributed in all the right places, but her back had gone a little soft, bulging a bit above the top seam of the halter.

She'd cut her hair, too. Real short, almost mannish. And when she turned, Katz saw the looseness around her jaw, the beginnings of a double chin. Pale, as always. Downright pallid in the sickly light of the bar, but none of that mattered. Men flocked to her: They always had and always would. And not because she was loose. She wasn't. In some ways, she was the pickiest woman Katz had ever known.

Maybe it was her unpredictability.

Her body, full and curvy and, let's face it, flabby, managed to convey an intoxicating sense of sexual promise, and whether or not that would lead to anything was the big mystery. She'd been like that even when she and Katz were married.

That was it, he decided. Val was mysterious.

Screwed up, sharp-tongued, distant, plagued by bouts of low self-esteem exacerbated by genuinely low talent, but smart and funny and kind when she felt like it. A tigress when the mood hit her.

The guy on the right slipped his hand under her butt. She threw back her head, laughed, and dislodged him. Touched his nose briefly with a sharp pink fingernail.

Katz walked over and retrieved the shearling. He tapped her shoulder very lightly. She turned, then mouthed "You" over a high-decibel rendition of "China Grove."

There was no surprise in it. No irritation, either.

Just "You."

Katz flattered himself that she seemed happy to see him.

He held out the coat. Pointed to the floor.

She smiled, nodded, took the shearling. She slipped off her stool and laced her fingers between Katz's and stared into his eyes.

The fools at the bar looked stunned as she and Katz left.

Val didn't put the shearling on until they were outside and a half block from the Parrot. Her white shoulders were prickled with gooseflesh. Same for her cleavage. White breasts bouncing loosely. Katz fought the urge to put his arm around her, protect her from the cold and everything else.

As they walked, she said, "You're fantasizing, Steve."

He raised his eyebrows.

She stopped and stretched her arms wide. "Give me a hug. A big one."

He complied and they embraced and she bit his ear, whispered into it, "You look good, ex-husband."

"You, too, ex-wife."

"I'm a sow."

"Nothing like that at all. You women with your distorted body image—"

She silenced him with a finger on his lips. "Don't be nice, Steve. I might go home with you."

He drew back and looked into her deep brown eyes. A couple of zits occupied the space between her plucked brows. New wrinkles creased the corners of the eyes. His eyes took in all of it, but his brain registered none of it. All he saw was mystery.

They resumed walking. "Would that be a tragedy?" he said.

"What?"

"Coming home with me."

"Probably," she said. "Let's not find out."

She walked faster, breathing through her mouth and blowing out steam. He caught up. They reached the park in the center of the Plaza. On warm nights, kids, sometimes drunk and often rowdy, hung out here. Occasionally, the homeless occupied the benches until the uniforms cleared everyone away. Tonight it was devoid of human occupation other than the two of them. The Plaza sparkled with Christmas lights, silver-blue snowdrifts, hundreds of white diamond stars, and pure magic. Too much cheer for a man who lived in a granite yard. Katz felt suddenly depressed.

Valerie said, "Is this about Olafson?"

"How'd you know?"

"Because Olafson's dead, and I know what your job is. What is it, Steve? Did my name show up somewhere?"

"In his Palm Pilot."

"There you go." She rubbed her hands together. "I could be a detective, too."

She sat down on a bench and jammed her stiff fingers into the pockets of her coat. "Here I was, sitting in a nice warm bar, getting nice warm male attention."

"Let's go inside somewhere," said Katz. "We could sit in my car, and I'll turn the heater on."

She smiled. "And neck?"

"Cut it out," he said, surprised at the anger in his voice.

"Sorry for offending you." She crossed her arms over her chest. Tight-lipped and colder than the air.

"Sorry," he said. "I've been working twenty-four hours with almost no sleep."

"All that's your decision, Steve."

"I'm sorry, Val. Okay? Let's start from scratch."

"Sure," she said. "And while we're at it, let's have world peace." She turned, studied him, and gave him a look that made him wonder if she was going to cry. What now?

"Val—"

"Been out to Bandelier recently, Steve?"

"Not recently," he said. Sometimes on days off, he drove out to the national park and got waved in free by the ranger: courtesy from one uniform to another. When tourists were there, he hiked. On slow days, he climbed a ladder up to one of the ancient Anasazi caves and just sat, staring at the ruins of the old pueblo marketplace below. Two Moons would have laughed, but Katz truly felt at one with the spirits of the land. He'd discovered the park right after the divorce, driving aimlessly, exploring the wilderness. Unlike the Big Apple, New Mexico was replete with open space.

He hadn't recalled telling Valerie of his trips to Bandelier. But then again, he didn't remember too clearly what they *had* actually talked about.

They sat there on the bench for what seemed like a long time. Then, suddenly, she took his face in her frigid hands and kissed him hard. Cool lips but a warm tongue.

When she pulled away, she said, "Let's go to my place."

• • •

104

Val got her VW van from behind the gallery, and he followed her erratic driving to her studio apartment on an unmarked alley off Paseo de Peralta, not too far from the site of the murder. She lived in the guesthouse of a large adobe estate owned by a California couple who rarely made it to Santa Fe. Val was expected to take care of minor repairs. For the most part, she had the coyote-fenced two-acre property to herself. Once, she'd brought Katz into the main house and they made love on the owners' big pine four-poster, surrounded by pictures of the owners' kids. Afterward, he'd started to clean up, but she told him to stop, said she'd take care of it later.

They parked next to each other on the gravel pad. Val had left her front door unlocked and she shoved it open. Katz quelled the reflex to lecture her and followed her inside, accepting the cold Sam Adams she offered. She sat down on her bed, and Katz tried to ignore the terrible abstractions that filled the space like blemishes.

She stood inches from him, got out of her clothes quickly, said, "What are you waiting for?"

A good question. It was hard and fast and great, and Katz had to clench his jaws so as not to scream.

Later, lying naked in bed, she said, "I was in his Palm Pilot because he wanted me."

"Oh," said Katz.

"Not sexually," she said. "I mean, that was there, too. Even though he was mostly gay. But not totally. There was a hetero vibe, too—a woman can tell. What he wanted was for me to leave Sarah and come work for him."

"Why?"

"Because I'm a genius." She laughed. "He was planning to branch out to Pueblo pottery. He told me Indian art was getting big on the East Coast. With his New York connections, he could triple the business Sarah does. He was also planning to go online. He'd use the auction services for the cheaper stuff and get on the art sites for the higher-end, as well as do some advertising on his own site. He had plans to really build up the market. He said within a year, Sarah would be hurting and that six months after that, she'd be finished."

"Nice guy."

"Terrible guy." Val traced a circle around Katz's left nipple. "I think that was the primary appeal for him. Not just succeeding but causing Sarah to fail."

"What was your incentive to leave?"

"Fifty percent raise and eventual partnership. The raise I figured he'd come through with, at least in the beginning. The partnership was bullshit. He'd use me to get established, then get rid of me and bring in some lackey."

"You turned him down."

"I told him I'd think about it. Then I proceeded to ignore him." She played with Katz's mustache. "A week later, he called me. I didn't return the call. A few days after that, he called again. I told him I was still thinking about it. He got a little huffy, obviously used to having his way. The third call didn't come until two weeks later. I told him I was busy with a customer, would get back to him. When I did, he started off all indignant. Didn't I know who he *was*? Didn't I know what he had the power to *do* to me?"

She lay back, her heavy breasts flattened and spread. "I didn't play his game. I stayed really sweet and said I'd considered his very generous offer and would continue to consider it but for the time being, I couldn't commit. He was so shocked he just hung up without saying a word.

Soon after, I saw him walking in the Plaza right toward me. He saw me, too, and crossed the street."

"Why didn't you just tell him no?"

She smiled. "You know me, Steve. You know how I am with men."

She cooked up some spaghetti and tofu sausage, and the two of them ate silently. As Katz washed the dishes, he saw her yawn conspicuously.

He got out of the robe she'd brought him—one of his old ones, but the smell of other men permeated the terry cloth. It didn't bother him. He was just another man now.

He got dressed, then kissed her good night. Sweet and chaste with no promise about the future. He drove to the granite yard, figuring that tonight he might sleep okay.

9

Both detectives slept late and arrived at the station by ten. On their desks were identical messages—a meeting with Chief Bacon in an hour.

The session lasted two minutes: the chief asking what was up, Two Moons and Katz saying nothing so far. The victim had too many potential enemies.

"Does it look like we'll close it?"

"Maybe," Two Moons said. "Maybe not."

She thought a moment. "That wouldn't be great, but I don't think it'll have any ramifications. Either tourist-wise or citizen-confidence-wise. *Because* he had so many enemies, it could be seen as an aberration."

Neither detective spoke.

Chief Bacon said, "Not that I'm being pessimistic, guys. Okay, go out there and do your thing."

What *was* their thing? Two Moons was the one to ask.

Katz said, "Let's make sure the Skaggses' prints get checked out."

"Scheduled for tomorrow."

"Why not today?"

"You know those guys—there's always a reason." Two Moons got on the phone to the state crime lab and asked for a rush. He hung up, shaking his head.

"Rape case in Bernalillo's taking their time."

"Rape trumps murder?" said Katz.

"The victim was twelve, living in a double-wide with her drunk mother. The asshole crawled into her bedroom. Probably some former boyfriend of the mother's— lots of candidates in that department."

Katz told him Valerie's story about Olafson gunning for Sarah Levy's business.

Two Moons said, "Maybe Sarah bashed him." He picked up a pencil, let his wrist go limp, made a feeble chopping motion.

"Her husband could've," said Katz.

"Who's that?"

"Dr. Oded Levy. He's a plastic surgeon. He's also Israeli and served in the army over there. Plus, he's a big boy."

"Bad temper?" said Darrel.

"The times I've met him, no. But that's always been on pleasant occasions. You know . . . social situations."

"You socialize with surgeons?"

"Once," said Katz. "After Val started working for Sarah, Sarah invited her to a dinner party at their house. Val needed a date, so she asked me."

"Sounds like fun."

Far from it. Val had flirted with an orthopedist the entire evening. Soon after, she hooked up with the bone-jockey.

Katz said, "After that, I ran into him a couple of times. You know, like once you meet someone, you notice him. He always seemed like a mellow guy. He's younger than Sarah, by the way."

"And that means . . ."

Katz held up the palms of his hands and shrugged. "Nothing. That time at their house, he seemed pretty in love with her."

"She's a beautiful woman," said Two Moons. "I know how pissed I was after Olafson criticized my wife. No telling what an army-trained Israeli might have done, finding out that Olafson had planned to stomp out his wife's business."

Dr. Oded Levy's office suite occupied the entire ground floor of a medical building on St. Michael's east of Hospital Drive, due south of St. Vincent Hospital. The waiting room was empty and discreet, with butter-colored leather sofas and Indian rugs over wide-plank oak floors, copies of *Architectural Digest* and *Santa Fe Style* fanned out carefully on granite-topped tables.

Katz categorized the rock automatically. *Spotty ribbon gneiss.* Slabs of the stuff stood feet from his window at home.

A pretty receptionist greeted them. When they asked to see Dr. Levy, she stayed pretty and friendly.

"He just left for lunch."

"Any idea where?" said Darrel.

"The Palace," she said.

They drove to the Plaza, found curbside parking, then walked to the Palace Hotel. Dr. Oded Levy was sitting in the old Victorian dining room by himself, tucked away in a red leather corner booth, eating fried trout and drinking Diet Coke.

"Steve," he said. Even seated, his size was evident. Katz knew him to be six-four or -five, trim and broad-shouldered. He had tan skin and black curly hair cut short.

"Dr. Levy." Katz introduced Two Moons.

"You two must be working hard," said Levy. "You deserve a nice lunch." The doctor had the faintest of accents. His hands were the size of baseball mitts, with long tapered fingers manicured perfectly. His crimson silk tie was knotted loosely under a spread-collared sky-blue shirt. A navy cashmere blazer was folded neatly over the top of the booth.

"How do you know we're working hard?" said Katz.

"The murder of Mr. Olafson. It's all over the *Santa Fe New Mexican*. In the *Albuquerque Journal*, too."

"I haven't had a chance to read the paper," Two Moons said.

"Probably just as well," Levy said. "Also, Valerie told Sarah that you're working the case." Levy gestured to his right. Where the blazer sat. "Long as you're here, care to join me?"

"Actually," said Darrel, "we came to talk to you."

Levy's eyebrows arched. "Really. Well, then sit down and tell me why."

The surgeon resumed eating as Katz told him. Levy made a point of cutting his trout into precise squares, impaling the fish on his fork, and studying each bite before moving it smoothly to his mouth. When Katz finished, he said, "Last year he tried to buy Sarah out, and when that failed, he threatened to destroy her business."

"Any particular reason he'd have it in for her?" said Katz.

Levy thought about that. "I don't believe so. Sarah felt it was schadenfreude."

"What's that?" said Darrel.

"A German word," said Levy. "Joy at the suffering of others. Olafson was a power-hungry man, and, according to Sarah, he wanted to dominate the Santa Fe art scene. Sarah's established, successful, and well liked. For a man like that, she'd be an appealing target."

"Not pleasant, Doc," Katz said. "Some guy gunning for your wife."

"An interesting choice of words." Levy smiled. "Not pleasant at all, but I wasn't worried."

"Why's that?"

"Sarah can take care of herself." The surgeon ate another forkful of trout, drank some soda, looked at a wristwatch as thin as a playing card, and put cash on the table. "Back to work."

"Liposuction?" said Darrel.

"Facial reconstruction," said Levy. "A five-year-old girl was injured in an accident on 25. It's the kind of surgery I really enjoy doing."

"The opposite of schaden-whatever," said Two Moons.

Levy looked at him quizzically.

"Joy at the *recovery* of others."

"Ah," said Levy. "Never thought of it that way, but yes. I like that very much."

Leaving the restaurant, Two Moons said, "What do you think?"

"He's big enough," said Katz. "See the size of those hands?"

113

"His prints should be on file, too. State medical board."

They walked to the Crown Victoria, and Two Moons got behind the wheel. "Must be strange . . . putting together a kid's face."

"Impressive," said Katz.

A mile later, Two Moons said, "Be a shame to put a guy like that out of commission."

Back at the station, they called the medical board and put in a request for Dr. Oded Levy's prints. Processing and retrieval would take days. There was no way to fax the data directly to the crime lab.

"Unless we get the chief on it," said Two Moons.

"For that we'll need more."

"Levy's probably not going anywhere."

"You like him for it?" Katz said.

"Not really, rabbi. What about you?"

"At this point, I don't know what I like." Katz sighed. "This one's getting that smell. The reek of failure."

By day's end, they had a pleasant surprise, though a minor one: The techs had set out for Embudo to print the Skaggses, and the job was completed. The computerized scan had begun, and initial data would be in by five p.m. Any ambiguous findings would trigger a hand check by the lab's head print whiz, a civilian analyst named Karen Blevins.

Two Moons and Katz stuck around waiting for the results, taking time for a burger-and-fries dinner, clearing paperwork on other cases, straining to come up with a new avenue of investigation on Olafson.

At seven-thirty, they needed a new avenue more than ever: Neither Barton nor Emma Skaggs's prints matched any of the latents at Olafson Southwest or at the victim's house. Emma had visited the gallery, but she hadn't left her mark.

By eight in the evening, tuckered out and weary, Katz and Two Moons prepared to leave. Before they reached the door, Katz's extension chirped. It was uniformed officer Debbie Santana.

"I've been assigned to guard the gallery while Summer Riley paws through the inventory. It looks like she's got something."

Before Katz could speak, Summer came on the line. "Guess what? It *is* an art theft! Four paintings missing from the list."

Katz felt elated. A motive! Now all they had to do was find the thief.

"It's weird, though," Summer added.

"In what way?" Katz asked.

"There were a lot more expensive works that weren't taken. And all the missing ones were by the same artist."

"Who?"

"Michael Weems. Looks like she had a big fan. She's important—artistically speaking—but not high-end—yet. Larry was planning to take her to the next level."

"What's the value of the four paintings?"

"Around thirty-five thousand. That's Larry's retail price. He usually takes ten percent off the top automatically. That's not small change, but right next to the four Weemses was a Wendt worth a hundred and fifty thousand and a small Guy Rose worth a lot more than that. Both are still here. Everything *but* the Weemses is still here."

115

"Have you gone through the entire inventory?"

"I've covered at least two-thirds. There's an art-theft database. I could enter the information myself, but I figured I should call you first. Would you like the titles of the paintings?"

"Don't bother right now, Summer. We're coming over."

10

Merry and Max in the Pool, 2003, 36 x 48,
   oil on canvas, $7,000.00
Merry and Max Eating Cereal, 2002, 54 x 60,
   oil on canvas, $15,000.00
Merry and Max with Rubber Ducks, 2003, 16 x 24,
   oil on canvas, $5,000.00
Merry and Max Dreaming, 2003, 16 x 24,
   oil on canvas, $7,500.00

Katz and Two Moons examined the snapshots of the paintings.

"What are these for?" Darrel asked Summer Riley.

"We send them out to clients who inquire about the artist. Or sometimes just to clients who Larry thinks would be a good match with the artist."

Still talking about her dead boss in the present tense.

Katz had another look at the photos.

Four paintings, all of them revolving around the same subjects. Two naked, cherubic blond kids, a toddler girl and a slightly older boy.

Katz had seen them before. Dancing around the maypole, a larger canvas displayed in the great room of Larry Olafson's house. That one had caught his untrained eye. The subject had been rescued from tackiness because Michael Weems could paint. That Olafson was hanging Weems's work in his private space could've been a marketing ploy—taking her to the next level, as Summer had said.

Or could be he just liked her style.

So did someone else.

Two Moons squinted at one of the photos.

He frowned and Katz looked over his shoulder. *Merry and Max with Rubber Ducks.* The kids sitting on the rim of a bathtub examining the yellow toys. Full frontal nudity, a rumpled towel at the girl's feet lying across a green-tiled bathroom floor.

Katz cleared his throat. Two Moons slipped the photos into an evidence bag, handed them to Debbie Santana. He told Summer Riley to wait in the gallery office and led Katz out to the front room. The taped outline of Olafson's body remained affixed to the hardwood floor, and Katz found himself thinking *still life.* Imagining one of those little rust specks of dried blood to be the red-dot tag affixed to a painting, indicating that it had been sold.

Two Moons said, "What do you think of those paintings?"

"Never mind what I'm thinking," Katz answered. "You're thinking they're kiddie porn."

Darrel scratched the side of his nose. "Maybe *you*

118

think they're kiddie porn and you're doing what the shrinks say . . . projecting it on me."

"Thanks, Dr. Freud," said Katz.

"Dr. Schadenfreude."

Katz laughed. "Tell the truth, I don't know how I feel about them. I saw the one hanging in Olafson's house and I thought it was good—from an artistic point of view. You see four together, especially that one you were looking at . . ."

"The way the little girl's sitting," said Darrel. "Legs spread, that towel at her feet—we've seen it before."

"Yeah," said Katz. "Still, these are obviously kids Michael Weems knows. Maybe even her own kids. Artists have . . . muses. People they paint over and over."

"Would you hang that stuff in your house?"

"No."

"Olafson did," said Darrel. "Meaning maybe he had more than a professional interest in Weems. Maybe he dug the subject matter."

"Gay and straight and mean and twisted," said Katz. "Anything's possible."

"Especially with this guy, Steve. He's an onion. We keep peeling, he keeps smelling worse."

"Whatever he did or didn't do, someone wanted those paintings badly enough to kill for them. Which also fits with a nonpremeditated scenario. Our bad guy came for the pictures, not for Olafson. Either he tried a sneak-burgle, got caught in the act by Olafson, and there was a confrontation. Or he showed up and demanded them, and there was a confrontation."

"Makes sense," said Two Moons. "Either way, the two of them have words, Olafson's his usual snotty, arrogant self. He turns his back on the guy and *boom*."

"Big-time boom," said Katz. "Summer said Olafson sent out photos to anyone who expresses interest in an artist. Let's see who was interested in Weems."

Fifteen clients had received Weems mailings: four in Europe, two in Japan, seven on the East Coast, and two locals. They were Mrs. Alma Maarten and Dr. and Mrs. Nelson Evans Aldren, both with high-end addresses in Las Campanas—a gated golf-course and equestrian development that featured estates with spectacular views.

Katz asked Summer Riley if she knew Maarten and the Aldrens.

"Sure," she said. "Alma Maarten's a doll. She's around eighty and wheelchair-bound. Apparently, in her younger days, she was quite the party giver. Larry kept her on the mailing list to make her feel like she was still part of the scene. The Aldrens are a bit younger but not much. Maybe early seventies. Joyce—Mrs. A.—she's the one who's into art."

"What kind of doctor is the husband?"

"I think he was a cardiologist. He's retired now. I've only seen him once."

"Big fellow?"

Summer laughed. "Maybe five-four. Why are you asking all this? None of Larry's clients killed him. I'm sure of that."

"Why?" asked Two Moons.

"Because they all loved him. That's part of being a great art dealer."

"What is?"

"Relating personally. Knowing which artist fits with which client—it's like matchmaking."

"Larry was a good matchmaker," said Katz.

"The best." The young woman's eyes misted.

"You miss him."

"He had so much to teach me," she said. "Said I was headed straight for the top."

"As a dealer?"

Summer nodded emphatically. "Larry said I had what it took. He was planning to set me up in a satellite gallery, selling Indian pottery. I was going to be his partner. Now . . ." She threw up her hands. "Can I go now? I really need to rest."

"The kids in the paintings," said Darrel.

"Merry and Max. They're Michael's children. They're really cute and she captures their essence brilliantly."

The last few words sounded like art-catalog hype.

Katz said, "Where does Michael live?"

"Right here in Santa Fe. She's got a house just north of the Plaza."

"How about an address?"

Sighing theatrically, Summer thumbed through a Rolodex. She found the card and pointed to the street and address.

Michael Weems lived on Artist Road.

"Now can I go?" she said. In a lower voice, more to herself than the detectives: "Goddammit! Time to start over."

She was crying as she left.

Before they set out to talk to the portrayer of Merry and Max, the detectives worked the computer.

No criminal hits on Michael Weems, though ascertaining that fact hadn't come without confusion. A man with the same name was incarcerated for robbery in

Marion, Illinois. Michael Horis Weems, black male, twenty-six years old.

Two Moons said, "Maybe she had a sex change operation."

"Could be." Katz raised his red mustache. "At this point, I'll believe anything."

Michael Andrea Weems merited fifty-four Google hits, most of them reviews of exhibitions, almost all of those stemming from shows at Olafson's galleries in New York and Santa Fe.

Hit fifty-two, however, proved to be the exception that made both detectives stop breathing.

A small paragraph in the *New York Daily News,* and from the snippy phrasing, probably a gossip column rather than straight reportage.

Last year, a Michael Weems premiere heralding a dozen new Merry-Max paintings had been disrupted by the appearance of the artist's estranged husband, a minister and self-described "spiritual counselor" named Myron Weems.

The irate Myron had stunned onlookers by berating them for patronizing a den of iniquity and for "gazing at filth." Before gallery personnel could intervene, he'd dived at one of the paintings, yanked it off the wall, stomped the canvas, and destroyed the artwork beyond repair. When he tried to repeat the process with a second painting, onlookers and a security guard managed to subdue the ranting man.

The police had been called, and Myron Weems had been arrested.

Nothing more.

Katz said, "This feels like something."

Two Moons said, "Let's plug in Myron's name."

Five of the six hits were sermons given at Myron Weems's church in Enid, Oklahoma. Lots of mentions of "sin" and "abomination." A couple of direct references to "the filth that is pornography." The sixth citation was the identical *Daily News* piece.

"No charges filed?" Katz said.

"Let's check the legal databases," Two Moons said. "See if any civil suits come up."

Half an hour later, they'd found nothing to indicate that Myron Weems had been held accountable for his tantrum.

Two Moons stood up and stretched his big and tall frame. "He humiliates his wife, trashes her work, and she doesn't press charges?"

"Estranged-husband situation," said Katz. "That means they were in the process of divorce. The two of them could've had a complicated situation. Maybe the incident got bargained away for a better custody or financial arrangement. Or maybe Myron calmed down a bit. She's still painting the kids."

"I don't know, Steve, a guy's got deep convictions, something to do with his kids. I don't see him bargaining."

Katz thought, Welcome to the world of marital discord, partner. He said, "There's something else to consider. Myron had a relationship with Olafson apart from the art world. He'd helped Olafson deal with booze."

"All the more reason for him to be angry, Steve. He counsels the guy, and the guy showcases his ex-wife's work, pushing what he considers dirty pictures. Makes me kinda wonder how tall Myron is."

A call to Oklahoma Motor Vehicles answered that

question. Myron Manning Weems was a male white, with a DOB that put him at fifty-five. More pertinently, he was listed at six-five, two hundred eighty. They requested a fax of Weems's driver's license.

"If it says two eighty, it means he's three hundred," Two Moons stated. "People always lie."

The fax machine whirred. The reproduced photo was small, and they blew it up on the station's photocopy machine.

Myron Weems had a full face, bushy gray hair, and a meaty, cleft shelf of a chin. Tiny eyeglasses perched absurdly on a potato nose. Weems's neck was even wider than his face and ringed in front, like a twine-wrapped pot roast. The overall impression was a college football tackle gone to seed.

"Big boy," said Two Moons.

"Very big boy," Katz answered. "I wonder if he's in town."

When the detectives phoned Myron Weems at his house in Enid, Oklahoma, all they got was a machine. "This is the Reverend Dr. Myron Weems . . ." An oily voice that was surprisingly boyish. Weems's message ended with his bestowing a blessing for "spiritual and personal growth" upon the caller.

No response at his church, either. There were no records of Weems flying in or out of Albuquerque within the past sixty days.

Katz and Two Moons spent the next three hours canvassing every hotel in Santa Fe, expanded their search, and finally came up with a winner at a cheesy motel on the south side, just two miles from the station.

They drove over and spoke to the clerk—a Navajo kid just out of his teens with poker-straight black hair and a wisp of a mustache. Three days ago, Myron Weems had registered under his own name. He'd arrived in a vehicle whose Oklahoma plates had been duly listed. A '94 Jeep Cherokee, which matched the data they'd received from Enid. Weems had paid for a week in advance. The clerk, whose name was Leonard Cole, had seen him yesterday.

"You're sure?" Katz said.

"Positive," Cole answered. "The guy is hard to miss. He's huge."

Two Moons said, "And you haven't seen him since."

"No, sir."

Cole checked the clock. A television was blaring from the back room. He seemed eager to get back to his program. He took out a key and said, "Wanna check his room?"

"We can't without a warrant. But you could get in there if you were worried about something."

"Like what?" said Leonard Cole.

"Gas leak, water leak, something like that."

"We got no gas, everything's electric," said Cole. "But sometimes the showers get leaky."

They followed Cole to the ground-floor unit. Cole knocked, waited, knocked again, then used his master key. They let him go in first. He held the door wide open and stared into the room.

Everything was neat and clean. Four paintings were stacked against the wall, next to the made-up single bed.

Katz thought: A guy that big sleeping on that bed couldn't have been fun. Easier to do if you were motivated.

And the evidence of motivation was clear: A box cutter sat atop a plastic-wood dresser. The outermost painting was a shredded mass of curling canvas ribbons, still set snugly in its frame. Leonard Cole looked behind the picture and said, "They're all cut up. Pretty freaky."

Two Moons told him to leave the room and lock up. "We're sending some police officers by to keep a watch. Meanwhile, don't let anyone in or out. If Weems shows up, call us immediately."

"Is this guy dangerous?"

"Probably not to you." Katz took out his cell phone. "But don't get in his way." He called for uniform backup and a BOLO on Myron Weems's Jeep. Then he looked at his partner. "You thinking what I'm thinking?"

"I'm sure I am," Two Moons said. "Let's hit it."

Both detectives hurried toward the Crown Victoria.

All that anger.

The ex-wife.

11

The address matched a free-form, sculptural adobe on Artist off Bishop's Lodge Road a couple of blocks to the east, just before Hyde Park. It was only fifteen miles from the ski basin, and the air already smelled thin and sweet.

The place was illuminated by low-wattage lighting that gave hints of eco-friendly landscaping—native grasses and shrubs, hewn rock, and a girdle of snow-covered piñons. The walkway was a path of Arizona flagstone, and the front door was fashioned from old gray teakwood, the hardware copper with a fine old patina. No one answered Two Moons's knock. He tried the handle. Open.

Katz thought: Another one who didn't lock her front door. Downright stupid, in this case. The woman had to suspect her lunatic ex in Olafson's murder. He pulled out his gun from his hand-tooled holster.

Ditto for Two Moons. Holding his weapon with two hands, Darrel called out Michael Weems's name.

Silence.

They walked through the entry hall to the living room. No people there, but all the lights were on. High ceilings with beautiful vigas and latillas. The requisite kiva fireplace. The place was done up in style—weathered heavy furniture that wore well in the dry climate, softened by a few Asian antiques. Nice leather couches. Worn but expensive-looking rugs.

Too damn quiet.

There were no paintings on the walls, just bare plaster—off-white tinged with pale blue. Odd, Two Moons thought. But what do they say? Shoemakers' kids always go barefoot.

Speaking of which! *Where were the kids?*

Two Moons's heartbeat quickened.

Maybe they were sleeping over at a friend's house. Maybe that was *very* wishful thinking!

A pair of French doors at the rear led out to a shady *portal*. There was deck furniture and a barbecue on wheels, just like anyone's house.

Back inside, the kitchen was cluttered, just like anyone's house.

Photos of the kids on a stone mantel.

School photos. Merry and Max, smiling wholesomely.

Where the *hell* were the kids?

"Ms. Weems!" yelled Two Moons. His stomach started churning. He was thinking of his own children. He tried to push that thought away, but the harder he tried, the clearer their faces were. Like a goddamn Chinese puzzle.

Relax, Darrel.

His father's voice talking to him.

Relax.

That helped a little. He eyed Katz, cocked his head to the left, toward an archway to a corridor.

There was no other way for them to go without turning around. Katz watched his partner's back.

The first door to the right belonged to a little girl's room. He dreaded going inside, but Two Moons had no choice. He pointed his gun to the floor, just in case the kid was sleeping in her bed and hadn't heard them yelling. He didn't want any accidents.

Empty.

Not as good as finding the girl asleep but far better than finding a body.

The room was pink and frilly and pretty, with the bed unmade. Plastic stick-on letters on the wall above the headboard: M E R R Y.

Max's room was next door. Also empty. All boy, the place was a museum of Matchbox cars and action figures.

The last door was to an adult bedroom. Whitewashed walls, an iron bed, a single pine nightstand, and nothing else, including a body.

Where was she?

Where were the kids?

"Ms. Weems?" Katz yelled out. "Police."

Nothing.

There was another set of French doors on the right that led to a second *portal.* Two Moons exhaled audibly. Katz followed his gaze through the glass.

Outside, a woman stood in the hot white beam of a

spotlight, at a portable easel, painting. The handle of one brush in her mouth, another in a knit-gloved hand as she studied her canvas . . . appraising it, dissecting it. Behind her was a steep, snow-spotted hillside.

She let go with a series of dabs, then stopped for another quick assessment.

Katz and Two Moons faced the back of the easel. They were in full view of the artist, if she looked their way.

She didn't.

Michael Weems looked to be in her late thirties—at least fifteen years younger than her ex. She had strong cheekbones and thin lips and a sharp, strong nose. Good posture and long, slender legs. She wore a quilted white ski jacket over leggings tucked into hiking boots. Yellow-gray hair was tied back and twisted into a long braid that hung over her left shoulder. A black, fringed scarf around her neck. No makeup on her face, but she did have spots of sunburn on cheeks and chin.

Another one doing the Georgia O'Keeffe bit, thought Katz.

Two Moons rapped on the glass door lightly, and finally, Michael Weems looked up from her painting.

A quick glance, but then she resumed dabbing.

The detectives stepped out.

"You're policemen," she said, removing the brush handle from her mouth and placing it on a side table. Nearby was a tin of turpentine, a big pile of rags, and a glass palette ringed with circles of pigment.

"Sounds like you're expecting us, ma'am."

Michael Weems smiled and painted.

"Where are the kids, Mrs. Weems?" Two Moons asked.

"Safe," she answered.

Two Moons felt a weight lift off his shoulders.

"Safe?" Katz asked. "As in safe from your ex-husband?"

Michael smiled enigmatically.

"He's in town, you know," Katz said.

The artist didn't respond.

"We found four of your paintings in his motel room."

Michael Weems stopped painting. She placed her brush on the table, next to the pile of rags. Closed her eyes. "God bless you," she said softly.

"Unfortunately, ma'am, they're all destroyed."

Weems's eyes shot open. Dark eyes, dramatic against her pale hair. Hawklike and unforgiving.

"Unfortunately," she said. Making it sound like mimicry. She stared past the detectives.

Katz said, "I'm sorry, Ms. Weems."

"You are?"

"Yes, ma'am," Katz said. "You put a lot of work into those—"

"He was a devil," said Michael Weems.

"Who?"

She crooked a finger over her back and toward the hillside. A gentle downward slope of snowdrift, red rocks, piñon trees, juniper bushes, and cacti.

Michael Weems turned and walked to the edge of the *portal* and gazed down.

Scattered light allowed the detectives to see a shallow ditch running parallel with her property. Too small to be officially called an arroyo, it was more like a rut in the ground interspersed with gravel and weeds and rocks.

Just off center about twenty feet to the right was something larger.

A man's body.

On his back, belly-up.

An enormous belly it was.

Myron Weems's mouth gaped open in permanent surprise. One hand was splayed unnaturally, the other lay next to his tree-trunk thigh.

Even in the dark and at a distance, Katz and Two Moons could make out the hole in his forehead.

Michael Weems walked back to the side table and removed rags from the pile. Underneath was a revolver—what looked to be an old Smith & Wesson.

A cowboy gun.

"Cover me," Two Moons whispered.

Katz nodded.

Slowly, Darrel walked over, keeping his eyes glued on Michael's hands. She didn't seem perturbed or anxious even when he picked up the gun and emptied the cylinder of five bullets.

Weems had returned her attention to her painting.

Katz and Two Moons were now in a position to see the subject.

Merry and Max standing at the edge of a *portal,* both of them naked. Staring, with a combination of horror and delight—the delicious discovery of a childhood nightmare's falsity—at the corpse of their father.

Michael Weems aimed her brush at a circle of red on her palette, rosied up the hole in the brow.

STILL LIFE

Doing it from memory, without looking back at the real thing.

The rendering was perfect.

The woman had talent.

JONATHAN KELLERMAN is one of the world's most popular authors. He has brought his expertise as a clinical psychologist to numerous bestselling tales of suspense (which have been translated into two dozen languages), including the Alex Delaware novels; *The Butcher's Theater,* a story of serial killing in Jerusalem; and *Billy Straight,* featuring Hollywood homicide detective Petra Connor. He is also the author of numerous essays, short stories, and scientific articles, two children's books, and three volumes of psychology, including *Savage Spawn: Reflections on Violent Children.* He has won the Goldwyn, Edgar, and Anthony awards, and has been nominated for a Shamus Award. He and his wife, the novelist Faye Kellerman, have four children.

FAYE KELLERMAN's first novel, *The Ritual Bath,* won the Macavity Award and generated the internationally bestselling Peter Decker/Rina Lazarus series. She has also written the Las Vegas thriller *Moon Music* and a historical novel featuring William Shakespeare, *The Quality of Mercy.* Faye Kellerman's short stories have appeared in numerous anthologies, including *Deadly Allies, A Woman's Eye, A Modern Treasury of Great Detective and Murder Mysteries, Mothers and Daughters, Murder for Love,* and *The Year's Finest Crime and Mystery Stories.* Her nonfiction essay "How I Caught a Mugger" appeared in the bestselling compilation *Small Miracles.* She lives in Los Angeles with her husband, Jonathan Kellerman, and a rotating assortment of their children.